FRENCH CRIME FICTION

EUROPEAN CRIME FICTIONS

FRENCH CRIME FICTION

Edited by
Claire Gorrara

CARDIFF
UNIVERSITY OF WALES PRESS
2009

www.uwp.co.uk

British Library Cataloguing-in-Publication Data
A catalogue record for this book is available from the British Library.

ISBN 978-0-7083-2101-0

Printed in Great Britain by Antony Rowe, Chippenham, Wiltshire

Contents

Acknowledgements

In 2007, a British Academy small grant enabled me to complete research for this volume. I gratefully acknowledge the support of the Academy. Equally, I would like to thank the School of European Studies, Cardiff University, for help in the form of sabbatical leave, particularly colleagues in the French department who covered my absence. I am also very grateful for the expert assistance I received from the staff of the Bibliothèque des littératures policières, Paris, for this and related projects, above all library curator Catherine Chauchard.

In many ways, this volume was conceived at the Institute of Germanic and Romance Studies in April 2002 at a conference devoted to 'Cultural Intersections: Noir Fiction and Film in France and Italy', co-organized with Giuliana Pieri. I would like to thank Giuliana Pieri for her unwavering enthusiasm for this project and for the European Crime Fictions series which grew out of our joint interest in contemporary crime fiction. Special thanks also go to Shelley Godsland, our fellow series editor, and to Sarah Lewis, commissioning editor of University of Wales Press, who offered us the opportunity to develop the series and who has provided invaluable advice and guidance throughout.

Lastly, I would like to dedicate this book to the memory of Christopher Shorley, a much respected colleague and scholar of French studies.

Cardiff
April 2008

Notes on Contributors

Véronique Desnain is Senior Lecturer in French at the University of Edinburgh, Scotland. Her research interests are seventeenth-century French literature and theatre and women's crime writing in contemporary France. Her publications include: 'Les limites de la loi', *Supplément au bulletin de l'association nationale des études féministes* (2000), 'La Femelle de l'espèce: women in contemporary French crime fiction', *French Cultural Studies* (2001) and 'Elise ou la vraie vie? Reality and fiction in Brigitte Aubert', *Modern and Contemporary France* (2004). She is currently working on Sébastien Japrisot and the links between crime writing and tragedy.

Claire Gorrara is Professor of French Studies, Cardiff University, UK. Her research interests are in literary and cultural memories of the Second World War in France, French women's writing and French crime fictions. Her publications include: *Women's Representations of the Occupation in Post-1968 France* (Macmillan, 1998), *European Memories of the Second World War*, with H. Peitsch and C. Burdett (Berghahn, 1999) and *The Roman Noir in Post-War French Culture: Dark Fictions* (Oxford University Press, 2003). She is currently working on a project that investigates the relationship between French crime narratives and representations of the Occupation. Claire Gorrara is co-editor of two series for University of Wales Press: French and Francophone Studies (with H. Diamond) and European Crime Fictions (with S. Godsland and G. Pieri).

Simon Kemp is a lecturer at Oxford University and fellow of St John's College. His research interests are in the twentieth-century French novel, and include genre fiction and its pastiche, narrative form and the representation of the mind. Recent publications on French crime fiction include a monograph, *Defective Inspectors: Crime Fiction Pastiche in Late-Twentieth-Century French Fiction* (Legenda, 2006), an article, 'Les pièces à conviction: perception in French crime fiction and its literary influence', *Modern and Contemporary France*, 13 (2005), 149–60, and a co-edited volume, *Sébastien Japrisot: The Art of Crime*, to appear shortly.

Susanna Lee is Associate Professor of French at Georgetown University, where she teaches courses in the nineteenth-century novel, modern critical theory and religion and literature. She is the author of *A World Abandoned by God: Narrative and Secularism* (Bucknell University Press, 2006) and co-edited the 'Crime Fictions' issue of *Yale French Studies* (2005) with A. Goulet of the University of Illinois. Other publications on crime fiction include: 'These are our stories: trauma, form, and the screen phenomenon of law and order', *Discourse*, 25, and '*Au Bonheur des Ogres* and *Au Bonheur des Dames*: the dismantling of foundations in the *Série noire*', *Dalhousie French Studies*, 63. She is also editing the new Norton Critical Edition of Stendhal's *The Red and the Black*, to be published in 2008. Her book in progress studies the connection of narrative to moral authority in French and American twentieth-century crime fiction.

David Platten is Senior Lecturer in French and Head of Department at the University of Leeds. He has published widely in the fields of modern and contemporary French literature and film, including books and articles on Tournier, Djian, Verne, Artaud, Pennac and, more recently, on various *noir* writers, as well as on themes ranging from film in its social, political and cultural contexts to utopianism. A book on French crime fiction, entitled *Outsiders, Radicals and Storytellers: French Crime Fiction in the Modern Era*, is near to completion, and a new project investigating concepts of reading pleasure in the modern French novel is under way.

Christopher Shorley, who died in July 2007, was Senior Lecturer in French at Queen's University, Belfast. His research interests spanned a number of key areas of French studies and his work broke new ground in fields or subjects that are today considered canonical. He wrote the first monograph in English on Raymond Queneau (Cambridge University Press, 1983), and also had a keen interest in the visual arts (cinema, photography), *noir* fiction and music (particularly jazz). These interests are exemplified in his most recent book, *A Time of Transition in the French Novel* (Edwin Mellen Press, 2006).

Introduction

CLAIRE GORRARA

Crime fiction in a European frame

Into the twenty-first century, crime fiction stands as one of the most culturally significant genres of our times. The narrative patterns of crime and detection pervade almost all areas of cultural activity: from prose fiction, to film, television, graphic novels, computer games and the Internet. Writers such as Arthur Conan Doyle and Edgar Allan Poe, two of the founding fathers of modern crime fiction, are widely read more than a hundred years after they were first published, whilst more recent authors, such as Agatha Christie, Raymond Chandler and Dashiell Hammett, are considered by many to be worthy of entry to the pantheon of literary greats. Yet, despite the acclaim and popularity of such figures, the vast majority of the novelistic production associated with such a genre continues to suffer from what Peter Preston has described as 'a creeping literary apartheid', a form of discrimination that judges genre fiction to be inferior to so-called 'literary fiction'. In his article for the *Guardian*, Preston bemoans the fact that the organizers of prestigious literary prizes, such as the Man Booker, exclude crime fiction from their deliberations, decreeing that a large proportion of contemporary fiction is not worthy of critical attention.[1] As he caustically notes, such classificatory zeal narrows scope and leads to omissions that overlook some of the finest writers and their works: 'Booker world is cluttered with too many boxes, too many things that the judges discard.'

One of the purposes of this new series devoted to European Crime Fictions is precisely to open up such boxes; to look inside and to examine the dark contents of a form of fiction that has indelibly marked European culture. For if British critics and writers feel continually impelled to comment on the often meaningless labels that relegate home-grown crime fiction to the outer reaches of the literary establishment, then the over-whelming majority of other European crime fiction, read largely in translation, is cast even further into the wilderness. European crime fiction in languages other than English has received relatively little critical

1

attention in the anglophone world. Indeed, the somewhat ambivalent reception of European authors in recent years has generated controversy and a sense that an unacknowledged form of literary protectionism is in place. Such negative assessments seemed to be confirmed by the decision of the Crime Writers Association to change the rules governing the award of its coveted Golden Dagger for best crime novel of the year, a prize that ensures its winner increased sales and media exposure. With three European winners of the Golden Dagger since 2000 (Henning Mankell, José Carlos Somoza and Arnaldur Indridason), the organizing committee decided to exclude all non-anglophone contenders from future competitions with effect from 2006. In future, crime fiction translated into English from another language would be eligible for a separate prize. As former judge and critic Marcel Berlins commented acerbically, 'Johnny Foreigner need not apply'.[2]

In the academic world to date, there has been a comparable reluctance to recognize the distinctiveness and achievements of non-anglophone European crime writers. Standard companions to crime, detective and mystery fiction tend either to treat European crime fiction as an umbrella term, providing short generalized surveys of different national traditions,[3] or to view the whole notion of crime writing traditions outside the 'big two' of Britain and America as minor tributaries whose interest derives mainly from a select group of iconic figures.[4] In so doing, they give little sense of the cultural contexts from which such work arises. Of course, no companion or compendium can hope to account for the vast array of writing generated within the broadly defined notions of detective, mystery and crime fiction. Indeed, such a venture would flounder from its inception without a clear sense of the remit and parameters of its study. Yet works of this nature do indicate the need for a fuller examination of apparently 'interloper' European traditions and hint at the different formulations and manifestations of crime writing that they call forth. As Martin Priestman notes, the history of crime and detective fiction is 'multi-layered rather than unidirectional' and those layers take on a different coloration when played out in the highly individuated contexts of European history and culture.[5]

Yet it is against such an inauspicious critical backdrop that European crime fiction has developed as one of the publishing success stories of recent decades in Britain and North America. Specialist booksellers report sales of translated European crime fiction increasing fivefold over recent years, whilst smaller presses, such as Bitter Lemon, Serpent's Tail, Arcadia and City Lights, as well as specialist imprints such as Harvill/

Secker at Random House, have invested in new talent and promoted such fiction to anglophone readers in often innovative and media-savvy ways.[6] This upsurge of interest has been generated mainly by contemporary European writers, and above all by forms of crime fiction that engage in an incisive and highly politicized examination of social, political, economic and cultural transformations in Europe. The advent of a Mediterranean *noir* movement, for example, has generated much commentary, with authors such as Jean-Claude Izzo (French), Massimo Carlotti (Italian), Yasmina Khadra (Algerian) and Alicia Giménez-Bartlett (Spanish) credited with developing a 'literature of social inquiry'[7] whose primary function has exceeded literary entertainment to tackle the growing inequalities and criminal perversions that disfigure the countries bordering the Mediterranean, such as drugs trafficking, prostitution, terrorism, state corruption and political expediency, fraud, money laundering and economic exploitation.[8] In such texts, crime cannot be neatly compartmentalized but pervades and contaminates European cultures as a form of cultural currency that defies border controls and regulation.

It is this notion of the intersection of the global and the local that is one of the most persistent markers of European crime traditions into the twenty-first century, highlighting the myriad ways in which regional cultures and traditions are being slowly but irresistibly eroded by the growing internationalization of commerce and crime. Multinational corporations and international networks of criminality are often interchangeable in the pages of the contemporary European crime novel and their impact upon local communities is destabilizing if not fully destructive. These angst-ridden intersections have been well represented not only in Mediterranean but also in Nordic crime fiction.[9] The work of Swedish author Henning Mankell, featuring Inspector Kurt Wallander and set in the small town of Ystad, returns obsessively to Sweden's implication in ever-widening circles of international fraud, corruption and instability, such as the collapse of the former Eastern Bloc, the politics of apartheid and political assassination and the power of global capital.[10] Murder, violence and transgression function in the work of European authors, such as Mankell, as markers of startling shifts in lifestyle, customs and habits as individuals, communities and nations become ever more subject to global influences and imperatives. Crime narratives demonstrate how the door of Fortress Europe has been kicked wide open.

However, this notion of the shared traditions and concerns of European crime fiction should not be emphasized at the expense of divergent patterns and developments. For, whilst it would be disingenuous not to acknowledge the productive dialogues that play such a pivotal role in European crime writing, national and regional crime narratives have developed differentially and been both impelled and impeded by historically contingent conditions, such as the rise of fascism, the Second World War and the repressive regimes of communist rule. Such key historical junctures have had a seismic impact on European cultural activity and their imprint can be detected today on the variegated literary histories of crime fiction and the national preferences of readers, authors and publishers. It is in this context of shared influences and distinctive traditions that this introduction will now turn to the case of France and offer a brief survey of the cultural significance and historical development of French crime fictions.

French crime fiction: trends and traditions

From its inception as a popular literary form, French crime fiction has entertained well-documented relations with the literary mainstream.[11] From the narrative patterning of crime and criminality in the work of nineteenth-century realist novelists, such as Honoré de Balzac and Victor Hugo, to the work of some of the most accomplished contemporary literary practitioners, such as Jean Echenoz and Patrick Modiano, the conventions of detective and crime fiction have become a staple feature of the French literary landscape. Indeed, in recent years, it has become commonplace not only to acknowledge the textual innovation of some of the best French crime writers but also to consider an indigenous tradition of crime writing as a national treasure that should be nurtured and is fully deserving of academic study and support. The creation of the Bibliothèque des littératures policières in Paris in 1984, a copyright library, research and resource centre for all material relating to crime fiction published in France since the mid-nineteenth century, stands as testament to this national commitment.[12]

In terms of popularity, French readers, like their European counterparts, show a marked preference for crime fiction, both home-grown talent and translated fiction. It is estimated that crime fiction accounts for roughly 20 per cent of current book sales in France and a growing number of crime fiction festivals, round tables, literary salons and websites demonstrate the perennial appeal of crime fiction as a form of writing with which French readers engage as both an amusing pastime and a legitimate part of French cultural life.[13] Crime and detective fiction has also infiltrated the French education system, from individual examples of French

4

and Anglo-American crime and detective novels taught on the French school syllabus to university conferences and colloquia that signal crime fiction's growing importance in the academy.

The role of French authors and French culture more generally in inspiring and pioneering early forms of crime fiction goes some way to explaining why this popular literary form holds such cultural sway in France today. France was one of three national cultures, together with Britain and America, central to the development of detective and crime fiction as a distinctive narrative form during the mid-nineteenth century. This cross-fertilization of cultural influences can be detected in the very first narrative of analytical reasoning to feature a fully fledged detective, Edgar Allan Poe's 'The Murders in the Rue Morgue' (1841). For Poe's decision to situate his 'tale of ratiocination' in the dark and menacing streets of Paris with a Frenchman, the Chevalier C. Auguste Dupin, as the cerebral sleuth gestures at the importance of French intellectual and historical influences for his detective creation. Enlightenment principles of rational thought and deduction would be tested by a grisly double murder whose violence and ferocity echoed the bloody fervour and excesses of revolution and counter-revolution as mirrored in French history.

Poe's three short stories, featuring his infallible detective, sowed the seeds for the myriad permutations of crime, detection and resolution that would criss-cross Europe and travel the Atlantic over the next 170 years.[14] As David Platten explores in this volume, early French authors, characters and cultural mores played their part in moulding the fledging genre, one that in the case of France would be pursued in the pages of populist journals and newspapers in serialized format as editors realized the potential sales revenues to be generated by such narratives of crime and sensation, both true and fictionalized. Real-life figures, such as Vidocq, the informant turned police chief of the newly created Sûreté (the department of criminal investigations), titillated readers with the first of his lively memoirs in 1828, recounting his exploits on both sides of the law, and gave added impetus to an already well-developed French fascination with the figure of the criminal and his encounters with a feared French police, known for its 'surveillance, trickery and disguise'.[15] Emile Gaboriau's *L'Affaire Lerouge* (*The Widow Lerouge*, 1866), a melodramatic tale of children swapped at birth, pioneered the use of a novel-length investigative structure and introduced French readers to two of the most influential detective prototypes: the amateur sleuth and the representative of the police.

Following on from Gaboriau, French detective and crime fiction of the late nineteenth and early twentieth century was characterized by the creation of colourful super-criminals in the mould of Maurice Leblanc's Arsène Lupin, *gentleman-cambrioleur* (gentleman-burglar), a thorn in the side of the establishment with his feats of disguise and theatrical escapades, but also sympathetically portrayed in the build-up to the First World War as patriotic, even chauvinistic, in his promotion of French national pride and mastery in adventures such as *L'Aiguille creuse* (*The Hollow Needle*, 1909). It was also during these years that French writers, like those in America and Britain, would begin to set in place some of the 'puzzle mysteries' that would inaugurate a whole sub-genre of detective fiction, primarily those ingenious constructions of logic and artifice that called upon the reader to pitch their wits against those of the detective and, by extension, the author. The *roman d'enigme* or *roman jeu* as it became known in France is perhaps best illustrated by Gaston Leroux's *Le Mystère de la chambre jaune* (*The Mystery of the Yellow Room*, 1908) in which scientist and heiress Mathilde Stangerson is brutally attacked in a room locked from the inside and from which there is no other point of entry or exit. Introducing the teenage reporter-detective Rouletabille, the narrative contortions required to solve this much imitated 'locked room' mystery are deeply embedded in contemporary social, cultural and intriguingly scientific debates of the day, as David Platten discusses in chapter 1. Leroux's *chef d'œuvre* indicates the extent to which French crime fiction has often co-opted pressing public debates to enrich its intellectual literary endeavour.

Over the interwar period, French crime fiction, or more precisely francophone crime fiction, paralleled developments in anglophone traditions, seeking to perfect the gamesmanship of the detective fiction gauntlet thrown down to the reader. The creation of the detective fiction collection Le Masque in 1928 became a privileged outlet for such fiction and continues even today to symbolize this tradition of classic detective fiction in France. During the interwar years, Belgian authors of note, particularly Jacques Decrest, Noël Vindry and S. A. Steeman, began to make inroads into francophone markets in crime fiction. Their well-crafted narratives challenged reader expectations of the rules and narrative conundrums determining the who, when, where and why of crime and detection. In a French frame, novels by established authors and poets, such as Claude Aveline and his trilogy of Frédéric Belot mysteries, furthered the exchanges between high and popular culture that have been such a productive feature of francophone traditions. The 1930s were also a pivotal decade for French-language traditions in that they witnessed the creation of one of the most celebrated literary protagonists of the twentieth century: Georges Simenon's Inspector Jules Maigret, a creation examined in detail by Christopher Shorley in chapter 2 of this collection. Simenon's series, featuring the mild-mannered Parisian detective, would inspire both respect and imitation, above all for the psychological portraits of criminal characters and Maigret's intuitive methods as an empathetic presence, a seer of men's souls.

French crime fiction, like other European traditions, was brought up short by the events of the Second World War. With the defeat and invasion of France, the nation faced restrictions, rationing and a repressive regime of censorship which banned all American and British crime fiction and films as evidence of the decadent and degenerate spirit of those who opposed Nazi Germany and its allies. However, it was under such inauspicious circumstances that the first French-authored *roman noir* was published: Léo Malet's *120, rue de la gare* (1943), featuring the first French private eye, Nestor Burma. Malet adapted the now familiar tropes, metaphors and ambiance of American hard-boiled crime fiction to a French context. What in its American incarnation had been a troubling action-packed narrative of urban crime became, in Malet's hands, a darkly transposed image of life under German occupation. It was Malet's innovation to transfer such a 'foreign' model to the unstable, often terrifying, lived reality of his first readers, electrifying the narrative with the thrill of recognition, as the German occupation is recast as a tale of criminal intrigue, social breakdown and bloody murder.

In the aftermath of war and liberation, it was these 'dark fictions' that came to dominate the French crime fiction market and these are discussed in chapter 3. Such *romans noirs* were associated above all with a new collection, the Série Noire, launched by the prestigious Gallimard publishing house in 1945 and credited with introducing French audiences not only to the American and British classics of the hard-boiled school but also to talented new French writers who set forth an impassioned social critique of their times. Using both American and French pseudonyms, as well as writing under their own names, authors, such as André Héléna and Jean Meckert/Amila, tackled topics as diverse as the legacy of the war years, the abolition of the death penalty and the ravages of American-style capitalism. These voices, often positioned on the margins of French culture, set the French *roman noir* on a path that would make it synonymous with an investigative zeal and desire to uncover the excesses and abuses of those in power.

Yet this *noir* vision of society was not confined to prose fiction. It was also during the 1950s that a *noir* vision of society consumed by greed, passion and vice with little or no redemptive possibilities would be reflected in French film. French directors as diverse as Henri-Georges Clouzot, André Cayatte, Jacques Becker and Jean-Pierre Melville all come under the influence of *film noir*, a generic cycle of films that originated with largely *émigré* European film directors in Hollywood. Their angst-ridden visions of post-war society and its criminal outcasts came to symbolize the tortured conscience of France in the era of the atom bomb, the Cold War and rapid but uneven modernization. The productive cultural exchange between an American-inspired model and French adaptation would be a persistent feature of the many varieties of French crime fiction over the post-war period.

Building upon such *noir* visions, one of the most startling reconfigurations of crime fiction in France was the advent of the *néo-polar* in the 1970s. This was a highly politicized form of crime fiction that emerged in the aftermath of the revolutionary events of May 1968 in France. For if the social, cultural and political ideals of student, youth and worker protest appeared to have dissipated post-1968, leaving little recognizable trace, the French crime novel of the 1970s functions as one area of literary expression where a number of renegade left-wing writers continued to do battle against repressive social and political structures. Premier amongst these was Jean-Patrick Manchette whose work is examined by Susanna Lee in chapter 4 of this volume. Manchette's disabused crime novels can be read as both elegantly crafted mediations on the aesthetic (im)possibilities of crime fiction and as violent witty denunciations of the abuses of the bourgeois state and the insidious strategies used to keep its citizens in a blissful state of ignorance of their own oppression. During the 1970s and early 1980s, Manchette, along with writers such as Frédéric Farjardie, Pierre Siniac, Jean Vautrin and latterly Thierry Jonquet and Jean-François Vilar, transformed the form, politics and content of French crime fiction to reflect their sense of its possibilities as a form able to engage in a radical social critique of contemporary reality.

Into the 1980s and the 1990s, French crime fiction diversified as elsewhere in Europe and the *roman noir* increasingly become a vehicle for left-leaning writers with a social conscience, for instance Didier Daeninckx in novels such as *Meurtres pour mémoire* (*Murder in Memoriam*, 1984), a critical exposé of the intersecting histories of the Second World War and the Algerian war focused on the victims of state brutality and persecution. Other crime fiction writers, such as Daniel Pennac, with his Malaussène series of books set in the Belleville district of Paris, achieved international fame with fiction that appealed not only to crime fiction *aficionados* but also to the literary mainstream. Pennac's fictions and those of other writers of his generation can be viewed as forming part of a broader network of texts that have exploited the conventions of detective and crime fiction for literary effect, including avant-garde French stylists, such as Alain Robbe-Grillet and Georges Perec. As Simon Kemp argues persuasively in chapter 6 of this volume, such exchanges between 'high' and 'popular' culture contest often ingrained views of crime fiction as mass-produced formula fiction and offer instead a vision of the aesthetic possibilities of crime fiction as a protean literary form.

It is also during the 1990s that critical recognition was finally accorded French women crime writers. The visibility of French women writers in terms of both sales and media profile in the 1990s should by no means be interpreted to imply that women had been absent as writers of French detective and crime fiction until this point. Rather, they had been consistently marginalized, both individually and as a group, by series editors, publishers and the various literary gatekeepers of crime fiction. As Véronique Desnain explores in chapter 5 of this volume, women crime writers in France have a distinguished tradition of crime writing, even if both they and their readers have been uncomfortable with the notion of a clearly delineated body of writing that is gendered in nature. Yet the emergence of female-identified and even feminist issues in their fiction in recent decades has made a major contribution to ongoing debates over the representation of women in crime fiction, as well as the depiction of sexualized violence and victimization more generally. During the 1990s, women authors, such as Maud Tabachnik, Andrea H. Japp, Brigitte Aubert, Sophie Granotier and Dominique Manotti, chose to concentrate on crime and its aftermath and to focus above all on the ways in which society and the institutions of law and order have perceived, interpreted and judged the victims and perpetrators of violence.

Into the first decade of the twenty-first century, therefore, a compelling case can be made for French crime fiction as a cultural narrative fully embedded in its times. French crime fiction can draw on a substantial historical pedigree and set of traditions specific to its national context. Yet it has also flourished and developed due to its connections with its Anglo-American competitors, as well as a rich network of European influences that have coalesced in recent years on the concept of a Mediterranean tradition. As the product of both indigenous and transnational traditions, French crime fiction is well positioned to offer the reader a potent and formidable narrative of modern times.

Contexts and choices

The purpose of this current collection is to further critical understandings of French crime fiction by means of a rich diversity of readings that illuminate the cultural significance of such a popular narrative form. Until recently, critical approaches to French crime fiction have tended to separate into two groups: firstly, those compendiums, guides and anthologies, mostly in French, that adopt a 'survey and select' approach, recommending what might be considered the 'best' in French crime fiction. Compiled mainly by crime fiction writers themselves or passionate crime critics, these invaluable studies provide a wealth of information centred on the distinctive world of crime fiction and its cultural practices. Secondly, our appreciation of the structures, forms and conventions of crime fiction has been enhanced by theoretically informed studies which approach crime fiction via the prism of well-established critical models, such as structuralism and psychoanalysis.[16] This work has helped to legitimize the study of crime fiction and to advance our understanding of crime fiction as a formative cultural narrative, able to accommodate a range of sophisticated literary-critical readings.

The aim of this present collection is to build upon these approaches by exploring questions of culture and context.[17] These may take the form of theoretical contexts, for example postmodern appropriations of crime fiction, as well as biographical and historical contexts that draw attention to the conditions of production of particular works and authors, such as Georges Simenon. The intersection between crime fiction and its sociocultural context is a major preoccupation of a number of contributions to this volume, investigating crime fiction as a means of apprehending and charting transformations in predominantly French metropolitan society – from the disruptions of world war and the *révolution manquée* (failed revolution) of May 1968 to the discourse and debates of modernity, scientific rationalism and the gender politics of the late twentieth century. In all chapters of this collection, the emphasis is upon a plurality of approaches and critical frames able to generate innovative and stimulating readings of a highly engaging corpus of material.

Yet, if this volume is driven by contexts, it is also subject to choices. Whilst representative traditions, authors and movements have determined the chronological ordering of the study, decisions have also had to be made over what to include and what to exclude from such a varied field of cultural production. This volume is, firstly, grounded in the study of prose fiction rather than in the plethora of other cultural media in which crime narratives could be said to evolve, above all in their contemporary manifestations. French filmic and televisual narratives of crime and detection deserve a volume of their own, whilst well-established genres, such as *film noir*, have already been the subject of sustained investigation.[18] Further work on graphic novels that adapt or mobilize the structures and conventions of crime fiction is an area ripe for future development but not the object of extended discussion here.

Secondly, if this volume is anchored in a particular body of writing, the contours of such writing have been determined by geographical location. The main focus is on European francophone writing traditions with a preference for showcasing debates that have animated metropolitan French culture. Crime fictions produced by francophone writers from outside Europe are developing only now as a field of critical inquiry but promise to yield rich results. In a recent article, Pim Higginson examines how the crime novel, as a markedly Western cultural form, has evolved into an apposite literary vehicle for addressing issues, debates and histories germane to French-speaking sub-Saharan Africa.[19] Higginson's work traces the 'trans-Atlantic circuit' that has shaped the development of the francophone African crime novel and charts the careers and trajectories of leading francophone exponents of the genre, such as Abasse Ndione, Simon Njami, Achille Ngoye and Mongo Beti. Equally, much work has yet to be done on crime fiction produced by French writers who are the children of immigrants to France from its former colonial Empire, for example Lakhdar Belaïd, whose *Sérail Killers* (2000) investigates the social fractures and conflicts generated by the Algerian war of independence and its bitter reverberations amongst second-generation immigrant communities in the north of France. Crime writing by those who are positioned as excentric to French culture, by virtue of either their ethnic origin or their geographical location, demonstrates the potential of such a transnational and migratory literary genre to cast a critical eye on the varied cultural, political and historical dimensions of contemporary 'Frenchness'.

In the final analysis, this volume has no pretensions to stand as an exhaustive study of such a diverse and widely travelled genre. The volume is born rather of the wish to dispel some of the more entrenched assumptions about French crime fiction and to recognize the narrative innovation and aesthetic appeal of a form that, in the hands of selected writers, continues to offer a rich and sometimes critical insight into French social and cultural life. It is to this end that an extract in English is included at the end of each chapter, giving a flavour of the writing under discussion and, it is hoped, whetting readers' appetites for more.[20] Select bibliographies and further secondary reading for each chapter complement such an approach, enabling the reader to explore a context, theme or writer in more detail, whilst an annotated bibliography concludes the volume with a comprehensive overview of secondary reading in French and English for those who wish to research the field more widely. Crime fiction is an important part of the cultural history of post-war France. As this volume demonstrates, in its myriad forms, it offers a privileged optic on French cultural identities, both past and present.

Notes

1. See Peter Preston, 'Genre specific', *Guardian*, 17 October 2005.
2. Marcel Berlins, 'If British crime writing isn't very good, why shouldn't a foreigner win the coveted Golden Dagger?', *Guardian*, 16 November 2005.
3. See the entries for 'European crime fiction and mystery writing' that encompass eastern Europe, France and Belgium, Germany, Italy, The Netherlands and Flanders, Nordic countries, Russia and Spain, in R. Herbert (ed.), *The Oxford Companion to Crime and Mystery Writing* (Oxford: Oxford University Press, 1999), pp. 139–46.
4. See 'Introduction', in M. Priestman (ed.), *The Cambridge Companion to Crime Fiction* (Cambridge: Cambridge University Press, 2003), in which Martin Priestman acknowledges the omission of 'any non-Anglophone fiction apart from the French and high-cultural', pp. 1–6 (p. 6). However, there is some indication that such attitudes are changing, for example Stacy Gillis's forthcoming *Crime Fiction* (Edinburgh: Edinburgh University Press, 2008) which promises to devote one of its three main sections to 'crime fictions, from Georges Simenon to Henning Mankell, published outside of the Anglo-American tradition' (promotional material, 2007).
5. Priestman, *The Cambridge Companion to Crime Fiction*, p. 6.
6. See 'The bloody foreigners: crime fiction in translation' tour when, in March and April of 2006, three independent publishing houses collaborated to bring six European authors and their translators to visit British audiences in the wake of the decision of the Crime Writers Association to limit the Gold Dagger award to books written originally in English.
7. Michael Reynolds, 'Introduction', *Black and Blue: An Introduction to the Mediterranean Noir* (New York: Europa Editions, 2006), p. 10.
8. In April 2007, Europa Editions, in collaboration with a number of cultural institutes in New York, organized an international literature festival in which leading exponents of the contemporary Mediterranean *noir* novel were invited to meet readers as part of the PEN World Voices festival.
9. For an overview of recent Nordic traditions, see Bo Tao Michaëlis, 'Scandinavian crime novels: too much angst and not enough entertainment?', *Nordisk Literatur* (2001), 12–17.

[10] See, respectively, *Hundarna i Riga* (*The Dogs of Riga*, 1992), *Den Vita lejoninnan* (*The White Lioness*, 1993) and *Mannen son log* (*The Man Who Smiled*, 1994).

[11] For suggested secondary reading relating to French crime fiction, please see the annotated bibliography at the end of this volume.

[12] See my 'French crime fiction: from *genre mineur* to *patrimoine culturel*', *French Studies*, 60/2 (2007), 209–14, for an overview of the development of critical responses to French crime fiction.

[13] See, for example, the annual *Festival du polar dans la ville* hosted by the town of Saint Quentin-en-Yvelines on the outskirts of Paris. Created in 1994, by 2006 the festival hosted over 120 events in eighty different locations from cafés, schools and restaurants to retirement homes and even private homes. See the festival website *www.polar.agglo-sqy.fr*.

[14] Edgar Allan Poe, 'The Murders in the Rue Morgue' (1841), 'The Mystery of Marie Rogêt' (1842) and 'The Purloined Letter' (1844).

[15] For an overview of early French detective and crime fiction, see Sita A. Schütt, 'French crime fiction', in M. Priestman (ed.), *The Cambridge Companion to Crime Fiction*, pp. 59–76.

[16] See, for example, Tzvetan Todorov, 'The typology of detective fiction', in *The Poetics of Prose*, trans. Richard Howard (Oxford: Blackwell, 1977), pp. 42–52, and Jacques Lacan, 'Seminar on *The Purloined Letter*', in G. Most and W. Stowe (eds), *The Poetics of Murder: Detective Fiction and Literary Theory* (Harcourt, 1983), pp. 21–54.

[17] The volume contributes to a burgeoning field of research in French cultural studies which has taken crime fiction and crime narratives more widely as its subject of inquiry. See, for example, the special issues: 'Crime and punishment: narratives of order and disorder', M. Atack (ed.), *French Cultural Studies*, 12/3 (2001); and 'Crime fictions', A. Goulet and S. Lee (eds), *Yale French Studies*, 108 (2005).

[18] For example, Robin Buss, *French Film Noir* (London: Marion Boyars Publications, 1994), and, more recently, French contributions to the edited volume, A. Spicer (ed.), *European Film Noir* (Manchester: Manchester University Press, 2007).

[19] Pim Higginson, 'Mayhem at the crossroads: francophone African fiction and the rise of the crime novel', *Yale French Studies*, 108 (2005), 160–76.

[20] The authors of the volume have tried to ensure that English-language translations of the French originals are noted wherever available. The English-language titles of such translations are indicated in brackets on the first mention of the French text and full details are provided in the select bibliographies that end each chapter.

1

Origins and Beginnings: the Emergence of Detective Fiction in France

DAVID PLATTEN

Anxious to establish the parameters of their arguments, critics sympathetic to crime fiction have time and again returned to the question of origins: how, why, when and where did this literary brand first emerge? It is a problem familiar to geologists who measure rivers. The exact source of the River Nile was for many years something of a mystery. Recently scientists in Peru claim to have discovered a new source for the Amazon. Much is at stake; not only the title of 'the longest river in the world', but also a boost to the tourist trade in Peru. However, where mineral sources may be elusive, literary sources for the crime genres proliferate. The Old Testament and Greek myths are popular starting points, the Genesis and Cain and Abel stories especially, and the story of Oedipus, more on account of the riddle of the Sphinx than the parricide. Classical and popular folklore, from the Arabian Nights to the legend of Robin Hood, are touted. In France it is often claimed that the eponymous hero of Voltaire's *conte Zadig* was the first to demonstrate clearly the advantages of deductive reasoning, when he determined the recent passing of the king and queen on the basis of traces left by a horse and a dog, though Zadig, of course, had no crime to solve. Francis Lacassin points to the investigation triggered by the crime, which, he argues, is elevated in the best crime fiction to the status of a quest, allowing analogies to be drawn with the Homeric and Arthurian epics.[1] Indeed, the narrative of investigation has been proposed as a key generic marker, since it constitutes the spine of most crime novels but need not feature at all in fiction that deals extensively with crime, such as Balzac's short story 'Maître Cornélius' or even Dostoyevsky's *Crime and Punishment*.

Crime fiction moves easily from one culture to the next. By the end of his career Georges Simenon, that most parochial of writers, was published in thirty-nine countries, with his novels translated into fifty-five different languages. Indeed, on the basis of figures published by UNESCO, Maurice Périsset estimates that by the mid-1980s Simenon was the most widely read of all living novelists.[2] However, the universality of the genre, ever more apparent in a shrinking world, should not disguise its fundamental vampirism. Crime fiction feasts on national histories and cultures, which are then reflected in its own image. The obvious example of this conundrum concerns the turn to naturalism manifest in the hard-boiled narratives of the American depression, a major epistemological shift within the genre that reverberated across continents. After the Second World War, when they became more readily available, French readers lapped up the novels of Hammett and Chandler and the market for American crime writing in translation has since held firm. In the world of the French-language crime novel, the impact of the hard-boiled model was initially evident in the publication of pale imitations, but more interesting offshoots grew rapidly. Writers such as André Héléna, Jean Amila and Pierre Siniac, whose identities were forged in the fire of war and occupation, chose the crime narrative as the ideal medium through which to present alternative perspectives on the history of their country. Their work is now classified under a different heading, the *roman noir*, a concept embracing any kind of crime fiction that actively engages with the world beyond the text. The reliance on a hard-boiled vernacular drawing on Dashiell Hammett's minimalist style is also a distinctive feature of the *néo-polar*, a 'school' of politicized crime writing that flared in the aftermath of the student protests in May 1968. At the core of the *néo-polar* and more generally the *roman noir* is the naturalist mode of the American hard-boiled crime story, adapted and used to express the particularly French experiences of the twentieth century: war on a gargantuan scale; occupation by a foreign power; decolonization; and the possibility of social and political revolution.

Intercultural generic shifts can tell only part of the story, however. In France, for example, they could not account for the intimate, creative connections between some crime writing and the evolution of popular dialects. Albert Simonin, author of the classic gangster novel *Touchez pas au grisbi* (1953), also produced a dictionary of French slang, and Frédéric Dard, the creator of San Antonio, was at the time of his death in 2000 credited with 20,000 neologisms. Other trends germane to the French crime novel emerged in counterpoint to developments in the Anglo-Saxon tradition. As the classic detective novel in Britain was transformed in the 1920s and 1930s into a formulaic, middle-class parlour game, in France Boileau-Narcejac, producing novels that would be later adapted to the screen by

Hitchcock and Clouzot, was laying the foundations for the thriller genre. With the publication in 1929 of Simenon's *Pietr-le-Letton* (*The Case of Peter the Lett*) the iconic figure of Maigret first appeared, a throwback to the superman detective in a new era of social and political realism; later, in the 1950s we witness the evocation of the existential spy in the work of Francis Ryck, in contrast to the glamorous figures who people the novels of contemporaneous Anglo-Saxon writers, such as Ian Fleming, Len Deighton and John Le Carré.

Over the course of its history the crime novel, like a river fed by its tributaries, has gained in breadth and density. This branching-off strengthens the genre but makes it more difficult to discuss in generic terms. Some of the current terms can lead to confusion. For example, *roman noir* refers not only to the modern wave of naturalistic crime fiction but also to the popular gothic novel of the nineteenth century associated with writers like Anne Radcliffe, Horace Walpole and Villiers de l'Isle-Adam, and *néopolar* has come to designate any crime narrative offering a negative portrait of contemporary society. As the genre has continued to proliferate, it has also been perceived as a means of infiltrating the literary 'high brow'. In the past twenty years, crime fiction has entered the debate over cultural legitimacy in France initiated by de Gaulle's minister of culture in the 1950s, André Malraux. Writers from crime stables, like Daniel Pennac, Tonino Benacquista and Fred Vargas, have broken the stranglehold of the academy, establishing themselves as literary hybrids, both mainstream authors with serious things to say and, incontrovertibly, crime writers. Moreover, their success has encouraged critical reappraisal of their many illustrious predecessors. Crime fiction is thus given to a generic pliability, which can accommodate an imaginative extravagance. It is this creative vitality that has ensured the longevity of the genre.

This chapter divides into three parts. The first charts the early history of the crime genres, emphasizing those environmental factors that facilitated its inception and development during the second half of the nineteenth century. The second focuses on outstanding works that initially defined the genre, with particular reference to Gaston Leroux's *Le Mystère de la chambre jaune* (*The Mystery of the Yellow Room*, 1908). It suggests that the popularity of the crime narrative that first impinged on the public consciousness in the era of Darwin and Nietzsche stems from its propensity to dramatize our fundamental human drive to understand our place in the world and the universe. Those impulses are channelled through the first detectives whose mastery of logic and reason is such that they are apparently able to explain the inexplicable. The final section spotlights the

French tradition of the social bandit epitomized by Maurice Leblanc's creation, Arsène Lupin. Lupin is a kind of anti-detective, a free spirit whose ability to manipulate reality at one level constantly befuddles the agents of a repressive society and at another challenges the rational and empirical certainties invested in the classical detectives.

The business of crime

Jean Patrick Manchette's description of crime fiction as 'une littérature alimentaire',[3] (potboilers), less apologetic perhaps than other 'higher' literary registers about its status as a commodity, recalls the fact that this was a genre that first impinged on the national consciousness during the Second Empire, France's first wave of consumerism that was to roll on into the Third Republic, from the mid-nineteenth century to the threshold of the First World War. Astute critics, aware that most people know intuitively what they seek when their gaze alights on the crime shelf at the railway station kiosk, have concentrated their attention on the process by which crime fiction established itself not only as a literary genre but also as a mainstay of the French book market. In this context the expression 'origins of the genre' is taken to mean the economic, social and cultural conditions without which it is unlikely that crime fiction would have established itself as a distinct literary genre. Some excellent research and sophisticated analyses have allowed scholars to piece together a comprehensive picture of this environment, so I shall limit myself to a brief discussion of the key determinants.

Crime fiction could not have existed in a feudal society. In his far-reaching study *Surveiller et punir* (*Discipline and Punish*), Michel Foucault identifies the emergence of the detective story as one aspect of a process in which the physical violence of crime and punishment was abstracted into a series of rational procedures.[4] Or, as Howard Haycraft put it in prosaic terms: 'So torture slowly gave way to proof, ordeal to evidence, the rack and the thumb-screw to the trained investigator.'[5] However, in the field of law and order, Enlightenment values were incorporated into the design of imperial power; the first Préfecture de Police (police headquarters) formed part of the Napoleonic Code. In 1811 the celebrated former crook, Eugène Vidocq, was nominated as the first Chef de la Sûreté (head of the department of criminal investigation) in Paris. Reported incidences of crime promptly soared, fuelling suspicions that Vidocq and his team, who were non-salaried ex-convicts acting on private commissions, engineered crimes which they then 'solved', thus putting any number of hapless innocents behind bars. With a rapidly increasing urban population in France creating the conditions for the emergence of a criminal underworld, the need for a representative, publicly financed police force was pressing. The author Honoré de Balzac estimated that in Paris during the Restoration there were, out of a population of 1.25 million, 20,000 'professional' criminals, facing a military garrison of roughly the same number.[6] In 1829, the year that Robert Peel founded the Metropolitan Police in London, uniformed *sergents de ville* appeared on the streets of the French capital, and in 1851, at the dawn of the Second Empire, all French police forces were placed under the authority of a national police department, the Ministère de la Police Générale.

Far from being welcomed, this piecemeal introduction of a national police force was regarded in many circles as an affront to civil liberties. Although, in the mid-nineteenth century, the science of criminology was in its infancy, for the first time information on individuals was now gathered and classified. With the invention in 1840 of photography, the technology existed that would allow written accounts to be accompanied by identifying images. Ronald Thomas argues that this monitoring of the population marked a shift in the model of French citizenship, which he links more broadly to a change that occurred during the nineteenth century in common perceptions of the nation. He suggests that what was once understood as 'a people', that is to say a community of independent citizens each of whom was expected to exercise his or her free will, gradually becomes 'the state', a centralized, bureaucratic system of order and law enforcement that could potentially come into conflict with the rights of the individual. To this epistemological shift in the political macrocosm corresponds a fundamental change to the way we perceive and interact with other human beings. As Thomas surmises, 'the "character" who generated and expressed the romantic spirit of the nation' gives way to the 'alienated bourgeois agent of the state'.[7] It is interesting to note, in the context of Thomas's argument, that the classic examples of early crime fiction depict amateur sleuths unencumbered by the state apparatus. By the start of the next century, readers' sympathies in France lay with free agents and subversives, such as Arsène Lupin and Fantômas.

The birth of the genre was also facilitated by a pre-existing literary infrastructure. In the 1830s, readers hooked on adventure, romance and intrigue subscribed in their masses to journals such as *Le Siècle* and *Le Journal des Débats*, which published in serialized form Alexandre Dumas Père's *Les Trois Mousquetaires* (*The Three Musketeers*, 1844) and Eugène Sue's *Les Mystères de Paris* (1842–3) respectively. The popularity of the *roman feuilleton* subsided somewhat during the Second Empire as the reading public was enthralled by the *faits divers*, accounts of real crime published in the newly established daily press.[8] Still, classics such as Paul Féval's *Les Habits noirs* in the 1860s and Ponson du Terrail's adventures of Rocambole in the 1880s were immensely popular. In 1866, *L'Affaire Lerouge* (*The Widow Lerouge*), regarded as the first crime novel written in the French language, was published in instalments in *Le Petit Journal*. Its author, Emile Gaboriau, was a columnist on the paper as well as being its star 'in-house' *feuilletoniste*. Thus, through the deeds of Gaboriau, who published five more crime stories before his premature death in 1873, crime fiction emerges as a hybrid literary genre combining the appeal of the *fait divers* and the popular adventure novel. Its readership, the masses of townsfolk, at once horrified and titillated by the *faits divers*, lay in wait. It was, however, a laborious process. For some, Gaboriau's work belongs more to the tradition of *le roman judiciaire* than *le roman policier*; with the latter the narrative of investigation has a crisper definition, whereas in the former it is submerged in extraneous detail. In *L'Affaire Lerouge*, the narrative of the investigation is a small part of the whole of a novel dominated by turgid digressions on the theme of social hierarchies. And in *Le Crime d'Orcival* (*The Mystery of Orcival*, 1868), arguably the most satisfying of his mysteries, the narrative is interspersed with unnecessary pen-portraits of minor characters, and any lingering suspense is blown away by a 160-page witness statement occupying the middle third of the text, which provides extensive details on the background of the culprit.

In the later decades of the nineteenth century a science of criminology begins to take shape. Alphonse Bertillon's *anthropométrie*, a system of measurements and calculations designed to provide physiological details of suspects, information that could be retrieved from a numerically based index, was described in 1883 as *la police scientifique*.[9] At the same time primitive lie detectors were being developed in America, and in 1894 the London police began taking the fingerprints of suspected criminals. In his pioneering study Régis Messac observes that these sudden developments in the observational sciences gave the genre an added impetus.[10] The public at large, in thrall to the impact of scientific discoveries on their lives and environment, was fascinated by the conjunction of crime and science.[11] However, the crucial piece of the jigsaw that saw the crime novel emerge from the hybrid form of *le roman judiciaire* is located in the fast-changing urban environment of the Second Empire. Paris, resculpted by Haussmann and adorned with arcades and emporia, had become a spectacle, a glittering phenomenon that demanded to be interpreted and understood. In this period the journalist, seen as an essential guide through the labyrinth of this new world, and his cousin the *flâneur*, the semi-detached observer of city life and aesthetic inspiration to Baudelaire, set about decoding the city. They are joined by a third figure that looms out of the shadows: the detective. All three belong to a new class of knowledge-seekers, interpreters of the new, industrialized, metropolitan world of modernity.

Engines of thought: the first detectives

In April 1841 an American journalist living in Philadelphia published in *Graham's Magazine* a short story set in Paris. Edgar Allan Poe's 'The Murders in the Rue Morgue' is widely accepted as the first detective fiction; whether or not it constitutes the source of the genre, the 'Rue Morgue' is undoubtedly its most significant milestone. In the years immediately following its publication in the United States pirated copies of the text appeared in Paris, before Baudelaire's translation was published in 1855.

The impact of Poe's story may be gauged by its reception in France. The Goncourt brothers, who were the arbiters of literary taste and cultural matters of their day, praised its innovatory qualities:

> Having read Poe, one is struck by the revelation of something that apparently had not yet occurred to literary critics. Poe heralds a new kind of writing, the literature of the twentieth century: the miracle of science, turning formulas into fables, a literature that is both all-consuming and mathematical. Imagination with an analytic punch ...[12]

However, what sets 'The Murders in the Rue Morgue' apart and signals a new literary paradigm is the organization of the narrative elements of the story. The reader accompanies the detective, C. Auguste Dupin, as he first reads the newspaper reports of the crime, then visits the location, before finally summoning to the premises, where the melodramatic denouement is played out, the only person other than himself who knows the truth of the affair. This backwards narrative of ratiocination focalized through the character of the detective is the second part of a dual narrative structure, in which the absent narrative of the crime gradually reappears in the pages relating the stages of the investigation, as if it had been written in invisible ink. The narrative thus foregrounds the workings of the detective's mind, a mind that in its mastery of the abstract principles of reason and deductive logic is superior to the norm. At one moment in the story Dupin embarks on a startlingly accurate reading of his companion's mind, demonstrating how the latter's reactions to external phenomena over a short period of time allow for the reconstruction of his train of thought based on the principles of association and contiguity.[13] A century later, the famous psycho-linguist Roman Jakobson showed how in articulating our relation to the external world we use metaphor and metonymy in much the same way.[14]

Dupin, the first detective, is first and foremost a mental athlete, a biblio-phile who wanders the streets at night, his mind uncluttered by the rudiments of daily existence. It is important that he stays in training. The application of reason and logic in the service of detection can, the narrator suggests, be simulated through participation in games; chess, draughts and especially whist, in which the player must also make deductions 'from things external to the game'.[15] In 'The Murders of the Rue Morgue' it is precisely these external features, the *outré* elements, which confound the police. The main features of the case – the atrocity of the murders, the 'peculiar and unequal voice', the absence of motive and the 'praeternat-ural' agility of the murderer – amount to a subhuman physicality which contrasts with Dupin's powers of ratiocination. Indeed, Dupin effectively solves the murders through the exercise of reason; it is only in the concluding section that a material clue, the tuft of orange hair, provides the evidence that allows him to establish not the identity but the species of the assailant.

Dupin's preference for abstraction contrasts with the method advocated by Sherlock Holmes to a sceptical Watson in the second chapter, entitled 'The Science of Detection', of Arthur Conan Doyle's 'A Study in Scarlet' (1887). The inquirer, Holmes asserts, must 'learn at a glance to distinguish the history of the man, and the trade or profession to which he belongs'. Priority is accorded by Holmes to the keen observation of material evidence:

> By a man's finger-nails, by his coat-sleeve, by his boots, by his trouser-knees, by the callosities of his forefinger and thumb, by his expression, by his shirt-cuffs – by each of these things a man's calling is plainly revealed. That all united should fail to enlighten the competent enquirer in any case is almost inconceivable.[16]

The seeds of Conan Doyle's concept of the art of detection as a by-product of empirical science had already been planted in the fiction of Emile Gaboriau, whose charismatic investigator, Monsieur Lecoq, was apt to draw diagrams of murder locations, inspect footprints in the snow and produced the first plaster cast. However, in *Le Crime d'Orcival*, Gaboriau exposes the potential flaws in such an empirically led system. The discovery of a woman's body in a stream bordering the estate of a local aristocrat, followed by a further discovery that the château on the estate had been ransacked while the servants were away celebrating a wedding, lead to the presumption that the *comte* and Mme de Trémorel – the woman in the stream is unrecognizable – have both been murdered by a gang of ruthless bandits. In contrast to the peremptory investigating magistrate, Lecoq reads the physical environment as if it were, to paraphrase Tom Gunning, a multilayered text.[17] His inspection of the interior of the château and the route from the building to the stream yields a long list of false clues, red herrings that have been placed deliberately to mislead the investigators. The extravagance of the staging is such that for Lecoq each clue says the opposite of what it is intended to say. Thus, the five wine glasses left on the dining table inform him that there may have been more or less than five people present, but certainly not five, the piece of cloth clasped in the fist of the corpse will have been planted by the assailant, and the multiplicity of Mme de Trémorel's wounds indicate that she was killed initially by a single blow. Like the clock with its hands set back and the unmade bed that has not been slept in, this 'désordre factice' (artificial disorder) is out of synchrony with the natural world.[18] The crime scene at Orcival has been constructed by an 'architect', who anticipates the arrival of the detective and attempts, however clumsily, to sabotage him. Thus, by showing the extent to which material evidence can be manipulated and by deriving a logical explanation of the disruption, Lecoq looks back to Dupin rather than forward to Holmes. Gaboriau's reader is already encouraged to distrust material reality, whereas for Conan Doyle the substance of existence is the premise for detection. In its early days, therefore, crime fiction questions the nature of detection, effectively suggesting two differing and potentially contrastive modes of operation that would appear to reflect the different philosophical traditions of Britain and France. These two methods are brought into sharp conflict in what, for some aficionados, is the finest work of crime fiction in the history of the genre, Gaston Leroux's *Le Mystère de la chambre jaune*.

The novel was first published in 1908. As his title suggests, Leroux adopted what by then had become a convention in crime writing, the sealed-room mystery. He planned to outdo Poe and Conan Doyle, both of whom, he felt, had cheated, as they had failed to seal their murder rooms securely; Poe's orangutan had swung through the window of the flat in the Rue Morgue, and in 'The Adventure of the Speckled Band' Conan

Doyle's swamp adder had slithered through the hollow bell-rope.[19] In contrast, it is soon established that the yellow room in which Mlle Stangerson is attacked has no means of egress. In other respects *Le Mystère de la chambre jaune* is faithful to the classical model of 'The Murders in the Rue Morgue', notably in terms of its narrative structure; at the end of the novel Leroux's protagonist Rouletabille, a cocky young journalist, explains to a fevered crowd packed into a courtroom the mystery of the yellow room, and the equally mysterious events that succeeded it, *in reverse order*. Where *Le Mystère* differs from both its predecessors – and this is in part a function of it being a novel rather than a short story – is in the heightened degree of suspense that is maintained throughout the narrative. Mathilde Stangerson survives the attack on her person in the yellow room, but it is soon made clear that her assailant will return.

Le Mystère de la chambre jaune is the most blatant example of a crime narrative endowed with ontological significance. Rouletabille's infallible method echoes the cardinal precepts of Descartes's *Discours de la méthode*, the fountainhead of rationalism and ultimate symbol of the French philosophical tradition. He is pitted against an adversary, the legendary sleuth Frédéric Larsan, who appears to be hewn from the empirical rock of the Anglo-Saxon tradition, epitomized in the context of the crime novel by Sherlock Holmes. However, Leroux is not interested in a balanced presentation of this conflict. Larsan is depicted as little more than a superficial caricature, seen from a distance roaming the grounds of the estate apparently in search of clues. On the other hand, Rouletabille on numerous occasions extols the virtues of his own approach. He proceeds, the reader learns, by doubting the veracity of the external evidence until such a time as it no longer contradicts a rational explanation of events: 'you have here, monsieur, the essence of my approach ... I ask not that the outward signs lead me to the truth; I simply ask that they do not conflict with the truth that has been revealed to me by the correct use of reason.'[20] In this story the value of empirical and forensic evidence is subordinated, through the character and actions of Rouletabille, to the abstract realm of Cartesian reasoning.

Furthermore the text manifests a perceived ambivalence in relation to the world of science and scientific inventions. The novel works on the basis of a conceit undermining the material stability of the world as we habitually encounter it, the idea being that someone or something may, at any given moment, vanish into thin air. The principal victims of the crime, Professor Stangerson and his daughter Mathilde, are famous scientists working at the cutting edge of their field, on what is described on several occasions as 'la dissociation de la matière par les actions éléctriques' (the disassociation of matter by electrical activity). Passing references in the text indicate that Professor Stangerson is in the vanguard of physicists working on atomic theory. He and his daughter would have belonged to a new breed of scientists, engaged in research on the nature of the universe that would lead to the framing of Heisenberg's 'uncertainty principle' in 1928 and the subsequent discovery of quantum mechanics in the early 1930s. Thus, as I have written elsewhere, the Stangersons would be complicit in the schism that rocked the natural sciences at the end of the nineteenth century, when faith in the material permanence of the world enshrined in the laws of Newtonian physics was lost and the way laid open for the development of the 'invisible technologies' that would dominate the science of the twentieth century.[21]

If Leroux provides sufficient information in the novel to justify the seriousness of the Stangersons' mission, at the same time their work is diminished by the context in which it is undertaken. The scientists live in a world of dotty superstition. Their immediate environment is furnished with clichés from the gothic classics: the building itself (a vulgar mishmash of architectural styles); the credulous old servant; the forest with the witch and her cat; an angry innkeeper with a seductive wife; a mysterious game warden. To top it all, Mathilde Stangerson is subjected to repeated assaults by an unknown person whose essential attribute, the ability to disappear at will, parodies the principles underlying her father's research.

Such gleeful absurdity forms part of a comic vein that runs through the narrative – and, interestingly, is brought out in Bruno Podalydes's 2003 film adaptation – leading the French critic Jacques Dubois to comment that 'we are dealing with a kind of pastiche laced with irony'.[22] There is a further irony suggested by Leroux's veiled discourse on modern science. At no point in the novel is the reader afforded any detailed insight into the nature of the Stangersons' work in the laboratory. Instead Leroux turns the principle of the *dissociation de la matière* (disassociation of matter) into a metaphor, in order to establish a rather scandalous link between science and superstition, and, secondly, to emphasize the crucial distinction in the modus operandi of his detective concerning the twin processes of observation and deduction. For Sherlock Holmes these two stages of detection formed a seamless continuum, whereas for Rouletabille the relationship is more problematic. Thus, in *Le Mystère de la chambre jaune* we end up potentially not with a classic detective novel but with the staging of the relationship between the mind and the phenomenon in the guise of a detective novel. Whereas the work of the real scientists is equated with superstition, Rouletabille's method acquires the status of a scientific theory, a theory that is challenged at several points in the text. This process culminates in the episode of the *galérie inexpliquable* (the mysterious gallery) (*MCJ*, pp. 146–69) which may be read as an experiment designed to test the validity of Rouletabille's method of detection. The latter's system of knowledge appears to fail, when the villain evades the trap that has been set, by once again vanishing into thin air. However, having comically drawn a 'circle of reason' between his own abnormally large temples, Rouletabille triumphs with a logical tour de force. The solution to the conundrum is mathematical and, as with the solution to the mystery of the yellow room, derives from a precise understanding of how the subject's field of vision is constantly mediated by the effects of time.

Le Mystère de la chambre jaune, which allegedly provided the stimulus for Agatha Christie's subsequent career,[23] is a great crime novel precisely because the discourse on the nature of detection enhances rather than inhibits the pleasure of reading the novel. Seminal influence though it may have been on the evolution of the genre, however, it may be argued that the brilliance of *Le Mystère* has, to some degree, distorted our perception of what crime fiction is and, more importantly, why we enjoy it.

Arsène Lupin: portrait of the 'anti-detective'

Marc Lits contends that crime fiction was accepted as a separate literary genre in France during the last decade of the nineteenth century. In support of his argument Lits cites the acclaim with which the translations of the Sherlock Holmes stories were greeted, and, conclusively, the number of inferior 'copy-cat' crime narratives that sprang up in the last decades of the century, with writers like Fortuné Hippolyte Auguste du Boisgobey, Xavier de Montépin and Eugène Chavette taking their inspiration from first Gaboriau and then Conan Doyle.[24] In the 1920s and 1930s a number of writers and institutions saw fit to expound on the methods and procedures for writing crime novels. These included Dorothy L. Sayers, the London Detection Club and the American writer Willard Huntington Wright, better known as S. S. Van Dine, whose twenty rules for the production of the successful crime narrative were adapted for use in 'murder party' games.[25] Basing his analysis on close readings of Poe's initiatory stories, François Fosca reduced Van Dine's instruction manual to eight fundamental principles of the crime narrative.[26]

The driving force behind such attempts to codify the genre is a desire to establish parity between the fictional detective and the reader. The crime novel should therefore entertain a kind of *glasnost,* a transparency of clues according to which information should not be withheld or hidden from either party. This somewhat dogmatic egalitarianism hinges on an interesting presumption, that the process of reading a crime story entails a certain kind of intellectual pleasure, analogous to solving a crossword puzzle. In practice, this 'game' principle has little bearing on what is for most people the reality of reading crime fiction. The better crime novels are apt to pickle the minds of most reader-detectives; in many instances the most alert and experienced of readers will be guided by intuition rather than any vicarious detection. As Robert Rushing surmises, they are 'simply along for the ride'.[27] What they may experience, however, is the thrill of the disclosure, as the full significance of what had seemed incidental to the plot materializes.[28] There is a further problem with the prescriptive model. As a cursory reading of any Maigret novel or, indeed, *Le Mystère de la chambre jaune* itself – in which the narrator Sainclair announces that the reader is to be granted the same access to the facts of the case as Rouletabille[29] – will show, the model is not justified by the text. Simenon's Maigret novels tend to the elliptical; at an advanced stage in the narrative of *La Tête d'un homme* (*A Battle of Nerves*, 1931), the commissaire warms his hands on his stove and recapitulates the main details of the case, providing some information in the form of a chronologically ordered list that is here divulged to the reader for the first time.[30] With *Le Mystère de la chambre jaune*, although it is true that, in the cases of Rouletabille's discourse on Mlle Stangerson's coiffure and Larsan's walking stick, important clues are typographically flagged, arguably the most significant, the news that the villain is long-sighted and was forced to risk a dangerous return to the victim's room in order to retrieve his pince-nez, is not registered until the denouement.[31]

Codes and conventions certainly play a part in what we understand crime fiction to be, but the history of the genre has shown them to be extraordinarily malleable, to the extent that crime fiction has emerged as part of a bigger picture. The Marxist critic, Ernest Mandel, argues that the modern detective story stems from popular literature about 'good bandits', notably Robin Hood. According to Mandel, this tradition of social protest and rebellion rooted in folklore and song found its way into the literary mainstream in works by authors of bourgeois or even aristocratic origin such as Cervantes, Defoe and Byron, before being distilled into a purer form of transgressive literature with the advent of crime fiction in the late nineteenth century.[32] From this perspective a key figure in the development of the genre is the real-life adventurer Vidocq, the villain turned hero whose career flourished in the post-revolutionary chaos of France. Julian Symons remarks that Vidocq had a 'tangible influence on writers during and after his life-time', notably Balzac who interviewed him on several occasions. The *Mémoires de Vidocq*, a ghosted autobiography published in 1829, perpetuates the myth of Vidocq as almost a supernatural being. A striking element of this myth was his propensity for using disguises. Symons reports that when in old age Vidocq paid a visit to London, *The Times* gave his height as 5 ft 10 in. 'when perfectly erect' (he was in fact 5 ft 6 in.) and added that 'by some strange process connected to his physical formation he has the faculty of contracting his height by several inches, and in this diminished state to walk about, jump, etc'.[33] Now the ability convincingly to alter one's appearance and maintain a disguise over a protracted period of time is common to the early detectives, especially Gaboriau's Lecoq and Conan Doyle's Sherlock Holmes. It is even more decisive in the case of Arsène Lupin, who, despite not being a detective for much of his career, remains the iconic protagonist of early French crime fiction.

The Arsène Lupin series ran from 1907 to 1939. It consists of twenty novels written by Maurice Leblanc, many of which, including *L'Aiguille creuse* (*The Hollow Needle*, 1909) and *813* (1910), have since been adapted for film and television. The books still enjoy healthy sales figures; in 2004 the series was reissued in two volumes by Omnibus, and all eighteen novels remain in print in Livre de Poche. A literary monument, the name of which has eclipsed that of his creator, Arsène Lupin belongs in a pantheon of popular French literature that would include Alexandre Dumas Père, Eugène Sue, Jules Verne and his contemporary Fantômas.

Each Lupin novel rejoices in startling, though often ingenious, plot twists, narrow escapes and cliff-hanging melodrama with smatterings of romance. The better novels tend to be driven in one form or other by puzzles or riddles, no more so than in *813* and *Les Huits Coups de l'horloge* (*The Eight Strokes of the Clock*, 1923), and the solutions to these riddles often occur at climactic moments of the drama. Lupin is promoted in the blurbs as a *gentleman-cambrioleur*, a debonair thief who, at various moments in his career, occupies senior positions in government or the police. In the mould of Mandel's 'good bandit', a moral purpose and good manners are prominent. Leblanc is careful to divest his hero of brutality, though he occasionally displays a ruthless streak. On only one occasion, in *813*, does he kill an opponent, and then he does so inadvertently, losing track of the vital four minutes that his hand is pressed against the epiglottis of a stiletto-blade-wielding killer; usually he relies on a unique pressure-point move to immobilize his foes.[34]

Arsène Lupin exists as a mythological figure in the fictional universe of Leblanc's novels, as an archetype to which much subsequent crime fiction in France habitually returns, and as a precursor of other glamorous outsiders in the world of popular fiction, notably James Bond. In terms of Greek mythology he combines the stealth of Hermes with the swagger of Zeus, whilst tilting like Hercules at the prospect of immortality.[35] In relation to modern popular culture he would resemble the man in black, performing impossible feats in order to be able to deposit the box of chocolates at the foot of the lady's bed. Thus, in the opening scene of *L'Aiguille creuse*, he is identified by his gestures as a stylish intruder, dazzling two nubile young ladies with his lantern before removing his hat and taking his leave with an arching bow.[36]

Seen in terms of the plots, the foregrounding of mysteries and narratives that seek their explanation and particularly the incidence of riddles and puzzles as the motors of the narrative, the Arsène Lupin series clearly belongs to the crime genres. Yet at the same time the fictions are more extravagant; Lupin is so much larger than life that he appears almost as a fantastic creature. The most interesting point of comparison with more conventional detective fiction, however, is once again the extent to which the process of detection involves some kind of speculation on questions of how we, as human beings, apprehend reality, although, in the Arsène Lupin stories, the boot is mostly on the other foot, and the detective, confronted by a constantly shifting material world, is rendered impotent. In this respect *L'Aiguille creuse*, a magnificent novel that echoes Dumas's *Le Comte de Monte Cristo* (*The Count of Monte Cristo*, 1844) is an exemplary text.

The great criminal in his pomp is confronted by a schoolboy detective, Isodore Beautrelet, described as a student of rhetoric who, in spite of his tender years, has already published a modest *oeuvre* entitled 'ARSENE LUPIN and his method, a calculated mix of convention and originality, followed by a comparison between English humour and French irony'.[37] Beautrelet bears more than a passing resemblance to Rouletabille, not only in his self-confidence but also in his tendency to expostulate on the best methods of detecting crime. His is a familiar refrain. Asked to explain his remarkable success, he responds:

> firstly I think, I try above all to establish the general principle of the case ... Then I imagine a reasonable, logical hypothesis that concords with this

general principle. And then, and not before, I examine the facts to see if they fit with my hypothesis.[38]

The mantra is repeated on several occasions in the early stages of the novel. However, whereas Rouletabille's setbacks in *Le Mystère de la chambre jaune* are systematically reversed, in *L'Aiguille creuse* Beautrelet's seemingly dazzling successes prove to be either temporary or entirely illusory. Unlike Rouletabille, Beautrelet operates in a fictional universe dominated by the conjurer's art of deception. The world of Arsène Lupin is always double. The authentic and the fake are interspersed and often indistinguishable, and Lupin's control over the material world is such that reality for the other protagonists appears unstable at best. The suggestion is that the material world around us may be a simulacrum of what we perceive as reality. The key motif in this compacted narrative, where one illusion is piled on to the next, is the baroque conceit of the *trompe l'œil*. Thus the chauffeur's cap turns out to be a replica, the four Reubens paintings in the house immaculate forgeries, and the artefacts and statuettes inside the gothic chapel in the grounds of the estate have been stolen and replaced by plaster-cast imitations, made to appear damp and mildewed like the originals.

Although Beautrelet successfully stymies the activities of Lupin's gang of smugglers, he struggles in this baroque world, where reason ultimately fails to tame the truth, which is 'too beautiful and too strange'.[39] Deceived by Lupin's impenetrable disguises, he fails either to question the motives of the kidnapped Raymonde or to comprehend fully, in terms of its scope and ambition, the design of the master criminal. The solution to the riddle contained in the title of the novel is found not in the immutable system of language, but in a brilliant feat of engineering which literally converts a natural aspect of the landscape into a façade. Halfway through the novel Beautrelet believes he has hit gold when he discovers the Château de l'Aiguille, which is located in the centre of France in the department of l'Indre, on the other side of the river from la Creuse. However, this 'Aiguille creuse' is a decoy. The 'real' one is in fact a needle of rock situated off the north coast of France at Étretat, which, many years ago, was excavated and converted into the secret residence of French kings and queens. Complete with hidden entrances and exits, this sorcerer's castle consists of circular rooms each superimposed on the other, in which a precious national heritage, including the *secret des rois de la France* (secret of the kings of France), is stored. The highest room, *la salle du Trésor* (the treasure room), contains some of the most valuable paintings in Christendom, and there the guardian of the keep, Arsène Lupin, is master of all that he surveys. Beautrelet, taken hostage by Lupin, effectively becomes the sorcerer's apprentice. As the policeman Ganimard clatters his way up the inside of the rock, Lupin and his party leave through the central retracting panel of a triptych and escape down a spiral staircase.[40]

If ever there is a literature that encourages its reader to indulge in flights of fancy, then it is the Arsène Lupin series. The spiral staircase becomes a ladder, at the foot of which is the upper chamber of a sea cave. Plato's Allegory of the Cave teaches us that our understanding of reality must always be conceptual; the spectators are fixated by the shadows on the wall of the cave, unaware that this physical effect is produced by light projected from the entrance of the cave. The local fishermen of Étretat know that the cave beneath the Aiguille is completely submerged at high tide. However, they do not know that it has a mobile ceiling, which is activated by the rising sea water; Lupin's gift to France. The sorcerer's party slip out of the cave in a small boat, gliding quietly behind a curtain of seaweed which obscures them from the view of the submarine that had been sent by the authorities to prevent Lupin from escaping via the sea.

Lupin's mobile ceiling does not illustrate a Platonic concept of metaphysics; rather, it is part of the different physical universe that Lupin has constructed. And it is what locates him if not beyond then in the outer limits of the realm of conventional detection, in which the one, indivisible, physical universe, governed by the laws of science, is put at the service of the rational mind. For its early practitioners like Dorothy L. Sayers, who saw the detective story as 'an Aristotelian perfection of beginning, middle, and end',[41] the appeal of the genre stems from its formal qualities. However, crime fiction has flourished over the course of the last century largely thanks to its permutations, of which Leblanc's Arsène Lupin series has been the first of many. Marc Lits describes the crime novel as 'an offshoot of popular literature that has flourished longer than the others, that has successfully resisted the ravages of time, a spiritual son of the serialized novel whose success has eclipsed that of his father'.[42] It has become increasingly clear that the crime novel not only fits within a broader tradition of popular literature, but that in the modern world it has acquired something of the essential, universal qualities associated with the traditional folk tale. Perhaps the addictive quality of the crime narrative is not especially related to the reader's wish to become reacquainted with familiar archetypes nor to a need for the natural order of things to be restored once again, but rather to a sense of excitement that within the pages of the novel one or more of those too strange, too beautiful truths that confounded Beautrelet could lie in wait.

Commentators down the years have sensed that crime fiction possesses some intrinsic literary value that sets it apart from the other popular genres, without defining satisfactorily what that value might involve. G. K. Chesterton once stated that it was the only form of popular literature 'in which is expressed some sense of the poetry of modern life',[43] and Sartre referred to Arsène Lupin as 'le Cyrano de la pègre' (the Cyrano of the criminal underworld).[44] None the less, the marketing of crime fiction today, with its cover designs, its star writers, literary fairs devoted to it and its own specialist academic journals, necessarily strengthens its generic boundaries and thus sets a stiff challenge for the would-be artists who have chosen it as the medium in which to express their talents. The budding crime writer must from the outset satisfy the expectations of a particular readership. It is a relationship that restricts the creative act of writing before it has taken form. As Poe once did in a dingy journalist's office in Philadelphia, the crime writer of today must constantly chip away at the coalface of literary invention.

* * *

Extract from Gaston Leroux's *Le Mystère de la chambre jaune*

This extract is from chapter 18 where Rouletabille ponders the events of the galerie inexplicable *and the escape of Mathilde Stangerson's attacker contrary to all expectations and his own careful planning. Rouletabille draws a circle between the two bumps on his forehead*
(Extract from Joseph Rouletabille's notebook, contd)

We parted outside our rooms with a melancholy handshake. I was glad to have awakened some suspicion of error in that original mind – extremely intelligent but entirely unmethodical. I did not go to bed. I awaited the coming of the daylight and then went to the front of the chateau. I walked around it and examined all the footprints coming to or leaving it. But they were so mixed and confused that I could make nothing of them. Here I should say that I do not as a rule attach overmuch importance to the external signs of crime.

That method, which consists in tracking down the criminal from his footprints, is altogether primitive. There are so many identical footprints. One may use them as an indication, but they can never be considered as absolute proof. However, that may be, in my troubled state of mind I went to the deserted main courtyard, looking for some clue to what happened in the gallery.

I must apply my reason! Desperate, I sat down upon a stone. What had I been doing for the last hour if not the most elementary work of the most ordinary detective? I had been looking for some mistake, like any cheap inspector, for some footprints that would make me say and think what they wanted me to say and think.

I felt that I was even more absurd – lower down the intelligence scale – than those detectives imagined by modern novelists, men who acquired their methods from reading the stories of Edgar Allan Poe or Conan Doyle. Ah, storybook-detectives who erect mountains of nonsense out of one footprint in the sand, or out of the impression of a hand on a wall! Their methods lead them to have innocent persons convicted and you, Larsan, are, after all, just another of those detectives!

You have been able to convince the judge, the Chief of the Sûreté himself – everybody. You need one final piece of evidence. Fool! You still do not have the very first! The evidence supplied by the senses only is no proof at all. I too am bent over superficial clues, but only to demand that they come within the circle drawn by my reason. The circle has often been very small indeed, But, however small, it was also immense, for it contained nothing but the truth. Yes, yes, external signs have never been anything to me but servants – they were never my masters.

Gaston Leroux, *Le Mystère de la chambre jaune*, revised and edited by Margaret Jull Costa (Cambs.: Dedalus Ltd, 2003), pp. 136–7.

Notes

[1] Francis Lacassin, *Mythologie du roman policier* (Mesnil-sur-l'Estrée: Bourgeois, 1993), pp. 23–8.

[2] Maurice Périsset, *Panorama du polar français contemporain* (Paris: L'Instant, 1986), p. 217.

[3] Cited in Uri Eisenzweig, *Le Récit impossible* (Paris: Bourgeois, 1986), p. 102.

[4] Michel Foucault, *Surveiller et punir: naissance de la prison* (Paris: Gallimard, 1975).

[5] Howard Haycraft, *Murder for Pleasure: The Life and Times of the Detective Story* (New York: Carroll & Graf, 1984; first published in 1941), p. 5.

[6] Cited in Ernest Mandel, *Delightful Murder: A Social History of the Crime Story* (London: Pluto Press, 1984), p. 5.

[7] Ronald Thomas, *Detective Fiction and the Rise of Forensic Science* (Cambridge: Cambridge University Press, 1999), p. 11.

[8] In a penetrating and exhaustive analysis, David Walker has shown how the language of the *fait divers* has since been incorporated into the fiction of an array of modern French writers. See David Walker, *Outrage and Insight: Modern French Writers and the 'fait divers'* (Oxford and Washington: Berg, 1995).

[9] For an interesting study on the literary applications of Bertillon's anthropometrics, see Nanette L. Fornabai, 'Criminal factors: Fantômas, anthropometrics, and the numerical fictions of modern criminal identity', *Yale French Studies*, A. Goulet and S. Lee (eds), 108 (2005), 60–73.

[10] Régis Messac, *Le Détective-novel et l'influence de la pensée scientifique* (Geneva: Slatkine Reprints, 1975; first published in 1929).

11 Jules Claretie's novel *L'Accusateur*, first published in 1896, plays on popular belief that the retina can capture the last image seen by a person before his or her death.

12 'Après avoir lu du Poë, la révélation de quelque chose dont la critique n'a point l'air de se douter. Poë, une littérature nouvelle, la littérature du XXe siècle: le miracle scientifique, la fabulation A + B, une littérature à la fois monomaniaque et mathématique. De l'imagination à coup d'analyse ...', cited in Uri Eisenzweig, *Autopsies du roman policier* (Paris: UGE, 10/18, 1983), p. 59. All translations of original French texts are my own. Free online English translations of *Le Mystère de la chambre jaune* may be downloaded at *http.// www.leroux.the freelibrary.com*, *http://www.online-literature.com/leroux/*, and *www.gutenberg.org/etext/1685*. An English translation of *L'Aiguille creuse* (*The Hollow Needle*) may also be downloaded at *www.gutenberg.org/ etext/4017*.

13 Edgar Allan Poe, 'The Murders in the Rue Morgue', in J. Symons (ed.), *Edgar Allan Poe: Selected Tales* (Oxford: The World's Classics Series, Oxford University Press, 1980), pp. 109–10.

14 Roman Jakobson, 'Aphasia as a linguistic topic', *Selected Writings II* (The Hague/Paris: Word and Language, Mouton, 1971), pp. 229–38.

15 Poe, 'The Murders in the Rue Morgue', p. 106.

16 Arthur Conan Doyle, 'A Study in Scarlet', *The Complete Sherlock Holmes* (Harmondsworth: Penguin, 1985; first published in 1930), p. 23.

17 See Tom Gunning, 'Lynx-eyed detectives and shadow bandits: visuality and eclipse in French detective stories and films before WW1', *Yale French Studies,* 108 (2005), 76.

18 Emile Gaboriau, *Le Crime d'Orcival* (Paris: Édition du Masque, 2005; first published in 1868), p. 84.

19 See Gaston Leroux, 'A mes amis d'outre-Manche', *Cahiers semestriels Gaston Leroux*, 2 (1978).

20 '[V]ous voyez, monsieur, quel est mon système ... je ne demande pas aux signes extérieurs de m'apprendre la vérité; je leur demande simplement de ne pas aller contre la vérité que m'a désignée le bon bout de la raison', *Le Mystère de la chambre jaune* (Paris : Livre de Poche, 1960), p. 253. Future references to this work will be signalled in the text by the abbreviation *MCJ*, followed by the page number.

21 See my article, 'Reading-glasses, guns and robots: a history of science in French crime fiction', *French Cultural Studies*, 12 (2001), 253–70.

22 'Nous avons affaire à une manière de pastiche au fil duquel l'écrivain pratique un mode ironique d'écriture', *Le Roman policier ou la modernité*, p. 161.

23 Agatha Christie wrote that it was whilst reading *Le Mystère de la chambre jaune* that she discovered her vocation, and Dr Fell, a character in a John Dickson Carr novel, described it as 'the best detective tale ever written'. See Julian Symons, *Bloody Murder: From the Detective Story to the Crime Novel: A History* (Harmondsworth: Viking, 1985; first published in 1972), p. 87.

[24] See Marc Lits, *Le Roman policier: introduction à la théorie et à l'histoire d'un genre littéraire* (Liège: Éditions du Céfal, 1999), p. 31.

[25] S. S. Van Dine, 'Twenty rules for writing detective stories', originally published in *American Magazine* (September 1928).

[26] See François Fosca, *Histoire et technique du roman policier* (Paris: Éditions de la Nouvelle Revue Critique, 1937) pp. 62–3.

[27] Robert Rushing, 'Traveling detectives: the logic of arrest and the pleasures of (avoiding) the real', *Yale French Studies,* 108 (2005), 90.

[28] See, for example, in later French crime fiction, the moustache of legendary Tour de France rider Fausto Coppi in Sébastien Japrisot's *L'Été meurtrier (One Deadly Summer*, 1979) or the toenails in the hotel bathroom in Fred Vargas's *L'Homme à l'envers (Seeking Whom He May Devour*, 2000).

[29] 'Vous allez donc tout savoir; et sans plus ample préambule, je vais poser devant vos yeux le problème de la "Chambre Jaune", tel qu'il le fut aux yeux du monde entier au lendemain du drame du château du Glandier' (You are therefore to know everything: without further ado, I will put before you the problem of the 'Yellow Room', such as it was presented to the world the day after the dramatic events at the Glandier château), *MCJ*, p. 10.

[30] Georges Simenon, *La Tête d'un homme* (Paris: Presses Pocket, Presses de la Cité, 1976; first published in 1931), pp. 127–31.

[31] See *MJC*, pp. 252–3.

[32] Mandel, *Delightful Murder*, p. 5.

[33] Symons, *Bloody Murder*, pp. 31–2.

[34] See Maurice Leblanc, *813* (Paris: Livre de Poche, 1966), p. 473.

[35] In Maurice Leblanc, *L'Aiguille creuse* (Paris: Livre de Poche, 1964), Lupin remarks that 'les années d'Arsène Lupin comptent dix fois plus que les autres' (Arsène Lupin's years count ten times more than those of others), p. 95.

[36] Leblanc, *L'Aiguille creuse*, p. 15.

[37] 'ARSENE LUPIN, sa méthode, en quoi il est classique et en quoi original; suivi d'un parallèle entre l'humour anglais et l'ironie française', Leblanc, *L'Aiguille creuse*, p. 56.

[38] '[J]e réfléchis d'abord, je tâche avant tout de trouver l'idée générale de l'affaire … Puis j'imagine une hypothèse raisonnable, logique, en accord avec cette idée générale. Et c'est après, seulement, que j'examine si les faits veulent bien s'adapter à mon hypothèse', Leblanc, *L'Aiguille creuse*, p. 64.

[39] '[T]rop belle et trop étrange', Leblanc, *L'Aiguille creuse*, p. 116.

[40] Leblanc, *L'Aiguille creuse*, pp. 205–45.

[41] Cited in Symons, *Bloody Murder*, p. 14.

[42] '[U]n surgeon de la littérature populaire qui a mieux réussi que les autres, qui a mieux résisté aux attaques du temps, un fils spirituel du roman feuilleton qui a dépassé la réussite de son père', Lits, *Le Roman policier: introduction à la théorie et à l'histoire d'un genre littéraire*, p. 37.

[43] Cited in Haycraft, *Murder for Pleasure*, p. 226.

[44] See Jean-Paul Sartre, *Les Mots* (Paris: Gallimard, 1964), p. 96.

Select bibliography

Claretie, Jules, *L'Accusateur* (Paris: Bibliothèque-Charpentier, 1896).

Conan Doyle, Arthur, *The Complete Sherlock Holmes* (Harmondsworth: Penguin, 1985; first published in 1930).

Gaboriau, Emile, *L'Affaire Lerouge* (Paris: Éditions du Masque, 2004; first published in 1866). *The Lerouge Case* (London: Dodo Press, 2007).

——, *Le Crime d'Orcival* (Paris: Éditions du Masque, 2005; first published in 1868). *The Mystery of Orcival* translated and available on line at: *http://www.gutenberg. org/etext/1651*.

Leblanc, Maurice, *L'Aiguille creuse* (Paris: Livre de Poche, 1964; first published in 1909). *The Hollow Needle* translated and available online at: *http://www.gutenberg. org/etext/4017*.

——, *813* (Paris: Livre de Poche, 1966; first published in 1910). *Arsene Lupin in 813* (Wildside Press, 2003).

——, *Les Huit Coups de l'horloge* (Paris: Livre de Poche, 1966; first published in 1922). *The Eight Strokes of the Clock*, translated and available on line at: *http://www.gutenberg.org/etext/7896*.

Leroux, Gaston, *Le Mystère de la chambre jaune* (Paris: Livre de Poche, 1960; first published in 1908). *The Mystery of the Yellow Room*, trans., revised and ed. Margaret Jull Costas (Cambs.: Dedalus Ltd, 2003).

Poe, Edgar Allan, 'The Murders in the Rue Morgue', in Julian Symons (ed.), *Edgar Allan Poe: Selected Tales* (Oxford: The World's Classics Series, Oxford University Press, 1980; first published in 1841).

Further secondary reading

Bayard, Pierre, *Qui a tué Roger Ackroyd?* (Paris: Minuit, 1998).

Boileau-Narcejac, *Le Roman policier* (Paris: Presses Universitaires de France (PUF), 'Que sais-je?', no. 1623, 1988).

Dubois, Jacques, *Le Roman policier ou la modernité. Le Texte à l'œuvre* (Paris: Nathan, 1993).

Horn, Pierre (ed.), *Handbook of French Popular Culture* (New York: Greenwood Press, 1991), 'Detective/ Mystery/ Spy Fiction', pp. 39–57.

Olivier-Martin, Yves, *Histoire du roman populaire en France* (Paris: Albin Michel, 1980).

Reuter, Yves, *Le Roman policier* (Paris: Nathan, 1997).

Todorov, Tzvetan, *Poétique de la prose* (Paris: Seuil, 1971).

Vanoncini, André, *Le Roman policier* (Paris: PUF, 'Que-sais-je?', 1993).

2

Georges Simenon and Crime Fiction Between the Wars

CHRISTOPHER SHORLEY

Simenon: a unique phenomenon

'The Simenon case' has been an indispensable reference in any serious discussion of crime fiction since the early 1930s. From reviews of the first Maigret novels to the classic 1950 Thomas Narcejac study, *Le Cas Simenon*, which enshrined the phrase, and on to more recent academic readings, it has always been clear that Simenon is a unique phenomenon in cultural, literary and publishing terms.[1] But his ready facility with forms and idioms, from lightweight potboilers to weighty meditations, his production rate and his commercial success – all without contemporary parallel – bring particular problems and contradictions. His status as an exceptionally popular writer has made it harder for him to be accepted and classified within the serious literary domain to which he aspired; and the sheer volume of his output, together with the endless film and television adaptations, means that his huge audience is unlikely to share a common corpus. For all that, his central importance and continuing presence are by now simply a matter of record.

In this chapter, a brief survey of precedents and predecessors will lead on to a summary of Simenon's life and career in general. Maigret is then examined in some detail, as a very special character and detective, after which there follows a broad account of the typical focus and manner of the Maigret novels – particularly those written in the first 'cycle', between 1931 and 1934 – and Simenon's very specific contribution to the crime fiction of the time. The chapter ends with a close scrutiny of one key example, *Le Chien jaune* (*The Yellow Dog*, 1931).

Precedents, predecessors and contemporaries

Crime and criminality had grown ever more prominent in prose fiction – French, British and American, among others – over the nineteenth century. They had a major impact on mainstream literature: in Balzac, through the melodramatic master-criminal Vautrin; in Victor Hugo, with the low-life, pre-Haussmann Paris of *Les Misérables* (1862); then in Zola's *Thérèse Raquin* (1867) and *La Bête humaine* (*The Beast in Man*, 1890), offering more modern images of moral and urban disorder. Similarly, in England, Dickens brought the London underworld to the page, as in *Oliver Twist* (1837–8). By general consent, though, a whole new genre reveals itself with the American writer, Edgar Allan Poe, whose 'The Murders in the Rue Morgue' (1841–2) both captures the feel of the contemporary urban world and establishes many durable *policier* conventions. Poe was soon translated into French and his influence spread rapidly, notably to Emile Gaboriau, in novels portraying systematic detection in a credible social and psychological setting. At this point, too, crime fiction was being serialized in the press, as in Eugène Sue's *Les Mystères de Paris* (1842–3). Soon after, from across the Channel, Conan Doyle's Sherlock Holmes became a massive presence, as both technical analyst and charismatic personality, and French translations appeared from 1902 – just before those of the New York detective and master of disguise Nick Carter.

Many vital elements of a French-language crime tradition emerged more clearly around the turn of the century, reaching an ever greater audience in the process. Maurice Leblanc's gentleman-burglar Arsène Lupin first appeared in 1907, like Gaston Leroux's Rouletabille, the journalist-detective; Leroux's lurid *Phantom of the Opera* dates from 1910, and his Chéri-Bibi, the innocent convict, from 1913. In a different vein, from 1911 the Fantômas series, created by Marcel Allain and Pierre Souvestre, mobilized a protean criminal superhero who inspired a huge cult following, for example among the surrealists, and who soon extended his mass appeal to the cinema. Generic features – especially the ambiance of mystery and suspense and the processes of detection – were well established by the end of the First World War and would soon be codified, by S. S. Van Dine and Ronald Knox, and decorously sustained by English writers such as Dorothy L. Sayers, with her aristocratic detective, Lord Peter Wimsey, and Agatha Christie, with her hyperrational Belgian, Hercule Poirot. The 1920s also saw the rise of hard-boiled fiction à la Dashiell Hammett, focusing on the corruption of American society and the tough guy protagonists who confront it.

It was towards the end of the 1920s that writing in French started to deal seriously with contemporary crime. From 1926, acclaimed writer André Gide recorded journalistic *faits divers* ('news in brief') and, later, accounts of trials – as in *La Séquestrée de Poitiers* (*The Prisoner of Poitiers*, 1930); and in 1928, to exploit the growing trend, the publisher Gallimard launched *Détective*, a mass-market 'great weekly magazine of *faits divers*' which recounted – and illustrated, through the lurid photography now available to the popular press – controversial murders and other major crimes. Within two years *Détective* had weekly sales of 800,000. Again, mainstream novelists played a significant role. Blaise Cendrars's novel *Moravagine* (1926) combines 'Poe-ish' undertones with the grotesque image of the murdered Mascha; Louis-Ferdinand Céline draws on the suburban squalor and aggression, typical of much subsequent fiction, in his period-defining *Voyage au bout de la nuit* (*Journey to the End of the Night*, 1932); and André Malraux, in the Goncourt-prize-winning *La Condition humaine* (*The Human Condition*, 1933), gives a very deliberate nod to Fantômas, and trades extensively off graphically described revolutionary conflict in the Shanghai of 1927.

The crucial developments, however, took place in a more strictly commercial domain. The 1920s and 1930s saw the creation of over sixty new series devoted exclusively to crime. In 1927, Albert Pigasse began the hugely successful Le Masque – and was swiftly emulated by publishers such as Fayard, Tallandier and Ferenczi, with symptomatic titles such as L'Aventure, Les Bas-Fonds and Dix Heures d'Angoisse. Le Masque itself, which ran to three hundred titles by 1939, began with translations of Anglo-Saxon authors, but quickly came to feature, for example, the prolific Belgian novelist Stanislas-André Steeman (1908–70), who, early in his career, co-wrote *Le Mystère du zoo d'Anvers* (1928), a pastiche of Leroux. Steeman's *Six Hommes morts* (1931) presented the sophisticated M. Wens, one among a number of contemporary protagonists who would successfully translate to the cinema. The intuitive Superintendent Malaise, another Steeman creation, was also a key figure and his 1939 novel *L'Assassin habite au 21* counts as an interwar classic. Other major figures also made their mark from this point on. Pierre Véry (1900–60) wrote *Le Testament de Basil Crookes* (1930), a poetic, Gallic variant on the classic British whodunnit, and then, from 1934 to 1941, a series centring on the lawyer Prosper Lepicq. Véry, who counted Malraux among his admirers, described these works as crime fiction with the colouring of *A Thousand and One Nights*, and wanted them to read as 'fairy stories for adults'. Among the major works of Jacques Decrest (1893–1954) is *Hasard* (1933), set in the world of gaming clubs, which introduces Superintendent Gilles, a subtle investigator explicitly sensitive to 'the human element' of criminality, which he would study in other worldly milieux. And Claude Aveline (1901–92), poet, playwright, travel writer, political activist and much besides, made a major contribution to both theory and practice with his Suite policière (1932–70), within which a note in *La Double Mort de Frédéric Belot* (1932) denies any meaningful distinction between popular crime fiction, on the one hand, and the literary novel, on the other, given that both depend on the same essential human qualities. The ambitions and scope of the genre were becoming gradually clear – and increasingly exciting.

Prevailing conditions during the Second World War, with the German invasion and the repressive Pétain regime, precluded access to authentic British and American writing. In 1943, however, Léo Malet, with *120, rue de la gare*, published what stands as the first *roman noir* portraying a credible historical reality, looking back to the 1930s, but set in depressed, occupied France, with its curfews, bombing raids and *vélo-taxis*. After the liberation, in September 1945, Marcel Duhamel launched Gallimard's Série Noire, which would, as his manifesto claimed, meet the needs of contemporary readers in search of an ambiance of amorality and pessimism, anxiety and sex, in a very 'un-Conan-Doyle-like' way, initially through translations of the Anglo-Saxons, but eventually produced by home-grown writers. From then on, a whole new configuration could develop.

However, from the upsurge around 1930 to the new departures of a decade and a half later, the dominant figure and the most significant trajectory were those of the Georges Joseph Christian Simenon – journalist, traveller and photographer, but above all novelist – who, well within his own lifetime, could claim to be the world's most widely read author.

Truth and fabulation, potboilers and literature

Simenon was born in Liège in February 1903. His birthday is often given as Friday 13 but also, sometimes, as Thursday 12, no doubt to avoid the other – fateful – date: an early example of the many ambiguities emanating from inconsistent interviews and contradictory statements in his memoirs, autobiographical fiction and the like. He was the elder son of Désiré, an unassuming insurance clerk, whom he revered, and Henriette, a tense, unstable mother who would always prefer her younger son, Christian. The family lived in the modest district of Outremeuse, identifying, as would Simenon the author, even as a sybaritic celebrity, with the simple virtues of commitment and hard work. He was a pious altar boy and a model pupil in his early schooldays and soon became a voracious reader of Gogol, Balzac, Dickens, Stevenson and Conrad – as well as the likes of Rouletabille and Sherlock Holmes. But with the First World War and the German occupation of Belgium he rebelled, becoming sexually promiscuous, thus establishing another lifelong tendency, and dabbling in petty crime, which would have obvious implications for his writing career. Subsequently he frequented a bohemian liégeois circle known as 'La Caque', which he would later commemorate in *Le Pendu de Saint-Pholien* (*Maigret and The Hundred Gibbets*, 1931). He had left school at fifteen, trying various odd jobs; but his future took shape from 1919, when he joined *La Gazette de Liège* as a cub reporter – and defined itself even more in 1921, when his first book, *Au pont des Arches* (*On the Arcade Bridge*), a would-be comic novel of Liège life, appeared under the name 'Georges Sim'.

The next major changes came in late 1922, when, after military service, Simenon broke with Liège – and Belgium – to move to Paris, and in March 1923 when he married Régine Renchon –'Tigy'– an aspiring liégoise painter who was to share his existence for three decades. After working as an office boy, then secretary to a right-wing aristocrat, he established himself as a writer of *littérature alimentaire* (potboilers) in the form of exotic adventures, comic sketches, mild erotica and more, mostly published by Ferenczi or Tallandier, and running to a total of nearly two hundred pseudonymous volumes between 1924 and 1933. And while these years hardly obscured his Belgian origins, they equally linked him more firmly with the writing profession in France. By the early 1930s, he was also gaining a reputation as a national and international journalist, producing extensive reportages on, for example, the little-understood controversies of colonialism in Africa (1932), the politically explosive Stavisky Affair (1934) and a spectacular six-month world tour (1935), as well as pulling off the scoop of interviewing the exiled Trotsky in Turkey in 1933. Another of his important – if less recognized – activities was photography: Simenon had learned camera techniques in the 1920s and complemented his journalism of the 1930s, such as his African reportage, with vivid and atmospheric images. During this period, he enjoyed a rich and hedonistic social life, with friendships with artists such as Jean Renoir and Maurice de Vlaminck, and numerous sexual liaisons (not reflected in the Maigret cycles), including a notorious affair with the black American dancer Josephine Baker, and his lengthy relationship with 'Boule', the Simenons' long-suffering maid.

Even before the end of the 1920s, travel was an integral part of Simenon's routine, as he moved around France and other parts of Europe by boat – first the *Ginette*, then the *Ostrogoth*, on which he did much of his writing. According to another perhaps apocryphal story, this is when Maigret really came into being, in late 1929. A vaguely defined 'commissaire Maigret', evolving from the 'pulp' detectives Jarry and Sancette, would figure in, say, the Marseille of *Train de nuit* (*Night Train*, 1930); and before long, in February 1931, an elaborate *soirée*, in the guise of a *bal anthropométrique* (anthropometric ball), complete with the taking of fingerprints and a decor of guillotines, launched *Monsieur Gallet, décédé* (*The Death of Monsieur Gallet*) and *Le Pendu de Saint-Pholien* (*Maigret and The Hundred Gibbets*). These novels, brought out by Simenon's newly favoured publisher, Fayard, portrayed a fully fledged superintendent, and bore the author's real name. But Simenon would later date the decisive transition back to September 1929, when he wrote *Pietr-le-Letton* (*The Case of Peter The Lett*), declaring that even if the text itself 'was not a masterpiece', nevertheless this move into the 'semi-literary novel' marked 'a sort of turning-point in my life'.[2]

It would be an exaggeration to claim that the first nineteen Maigret novels changed everything in Simenon's writing practices. Not surprisingly, he still resorted to some of the staples of popular crime fiction, such as the brutal violence in *La Nuit du carrefour* (*The Crossroad Murders*, 1931), the exchanged identities in *Monsieur Gallet*, or the Poirotesque summing-up, with all the suspects gathered together, at the end of *L'Affaire Saint-Fiacre* (*Maigret Goes Home*, 1932). Equally, though, with the advent of Superintendent Maigret, the genre was being freed of its more restrictive conventions and enjoying some much-needed fresh air.[3] By 1932, exactly when Aveline rejected rigid generic divisions, Simenon was making a similar argument.[4] And within a year or two he was already signalling another change of direction, literally pensioning off his already famous protagonist, in *Maigret* (*Maigret Returns*, 1934), and signing another new publishing contract, this time with Gallimard. Now, as he would explain to André Gide, he explicitly abandoned his detective and *meneur de jeu* (master of ceremonies): now he aimed to write a whole new strain of *romans durs* (serious novels) in which crime and investigation could give place to the closer scrutiny of the essential *homme nu* (the human self), as in *Le Testament Donadieu* (*The Shadow Falls*, 1937), and explore wider issues such as colonialism *Coup de lune* (*Tropic Moon*, 1933) or anarchism *Le Suspect* (*The Green Thermos*, 1938). And by 1939 Gide was proclaiming Simenon as 'perhaps our greatest novelist'.[5]

Simenon spent the Second World War in France, writing as prolifically as ever, and returning to Maigret (for a new publisher, Gallimard/NRF, in

Christopher Shorley

1942) as well as continuing his *romans durs*. While he was not explicitly compromised by his wartime activities (unlike his brother, Christian, whom he saved by enrolling him in the French Foreign Legion), Simenon was keen for a fresh start after the Occupation and moved, with Tigy and their son, Marc, to North America. He would remain there until moving, with his second wife, Denise, and their children, to neutral, orderly Switzerland in the mid-1950s. From now on, the sustained success of the Maigret novels was paralleled by a plethora of cinema and television versions across the globe. A final shift of direction occurred in 1972, when Simenon withdrew completely from fiction writing, devoting himself to his dictated memoirs (the *Dictées*), which developed the autobiographical line of earlier texts such as *Pedigree* (1948) and *Quand j'étais vieux* (*When I Was Old*, 1970). He spent his final years, after the breakdown of his marriage to Denise and the suicide of his daughter Marie-Jo, with his last mistress, Teresa Sburelin. Simenon died in Lausanne on 4 September 1989.

Maigret

Previous heroes of crime fiction, from Vautrin to Poirot, had of course displayed their own inimitable personalities. But, whereas this often contrived to stress their charisma, and even eccentricity, Jules Maigret imposes himself rather by his carefully detailed and reassuring ordinariness. Physically tall and heavily built, he is seldom to be seen without his hat and overcoat, not to mention the inevitable pipe – which will all be as prominent on the screen as on the page. He lives in an apartment at 130 Boulevard Richard Lenoir, in the eleventh *arrondissement* in Paris, with his devoted wife Louise, in whose home cooking he delights. He works from his snug office, with its cast-iron stove, upstairs in the headquarters of the Police Judiciaire, at the Quai des Orfèvres, on the Île de la Cité. He is a regular at the Brasserie Dauphine nearby and enjoys the company of his professional 'family', including Inspectors Torrence and Lucas. He also displays considerable psychological depth, perhaps because of his resemblance to various real Liégois or Parisian policemen Simenon had known personally, perhaps because of the highly developed empathy between author and creation. At all events, his past is recorded in detail – in the course of an investigation, as in *Maigret Goes Home*, or more systematically, in *Les Mémoires de Maigret* (*Maigret's Memoirs*, 1951): origins near Moulins, in the department of the Allier, in central France; medical studies at Nantes, abandoned for financial reasons; gradual progress up the ranks of the Parisian police force to his present and enduring status – which changes little over forty years and scores of investigations.

However, this fairly ordinary Frenchman is, by any assessment, a quite exceptional detective – and this from the beginning of the first Maigret cycle (1931–4). Beyond the residual potboiler conventions, the world of Maigret is thoroughly established in the initial nineteen volumes. For some readers, admittedly, there are differences between the first cycle and the second (1942–72), which can be seen as less active and more philosophical than the perhaps simpler early works. There is also, arguably, more emphasis, in the second cycle, on Maigret's personal state of mind, as is suggested by titles such as *Maigret Afraid/Has Doubts/Loses His Temper*, which contrast tellingly with early ones such as *A Battle of Nerves* or *The Madman of Bergerac*. One leading critic, in any case, is tempted to see the first cycle as making up one complete text in its own right, embodying recurrent and characteristic patterns of crime and detection.[6]

One key issue is the element of police procedural. Simenon – and with him his protagonist – often affected indifference to formal and scientific methods, but he had been aware of them from his time as a reporter in Liège; and after the earliest Maigret novels the director of the Police Judiciaire showed him around the Quai des Orfèvres to help him avoid the most obvious technical errors. There are, accordingly, gestures towards forensic procedures, such as the diligent measuring of a footprint in *La Nuit du carrefour* (*The Crossroads Murders*, 1931); but more typically, as in *The Yellow Dog*, Maigret steers clear of technical operations. Here, when his young colleague, Leroy, tells him: 'I still don't quite understand your methods, superintendent, but I think I'm beginning to see …', an amused Maigret replies: 'You're lucky, my friend! Especially in this case, in which my method has actually been not to have one.'[7] Likewise, despite the residue of pulp devices, early Maigret plots regularly run counter to standard or readily plausible patterns: the 'murder' of Monsieur Gallet turns out to have been a suicide; the killer in *Maigret Returns* is merely an anonymous hit man, outside the circle of 'predictable' suspects; and various guilty parties, as in *Un Crime en Hollande* (*A Crime in Holland*, 1931), are never brought to justice.[8] Simenon also strains credibility by allowing his superintendent a questionable amount of geographical latitude, giving him investigations in the provinces (Fécamp, Reims) and abroad (Bremen, Liège), perhaps imitating Simenon's own peregrinations, when strictly he might have been expected to confine his superintendent to the Paris area. Further, Simenon is generally seen, in the Maigret texts, as downplaying the importance of the history and politics of interwar France. It would certainly be difficult to deduce from them the current key events or controversies, let alone to identify Simenon's own sympathies. At the same time, he offers an acute awareness of individuals and their social backgrounds: family, for example, in *L'Ombre chinoise* (*The Shadow in the Courtyard*, 1932), geographical situation in *The Crossroads Murders* or circles of friends in *La Guinguette à deux sous* (*The Guinguette by the Seine*, 1932). Moreover, he carefully places them in a well-defined contemporary context of trains and cars, telegrams and telephones, which enable rapid communications and information flow between Maigret's dispersed observation points and headquarters in Paris; the world of a Simenon novel has smooth logistical underpinning.

Distinctive patterns can readily be discerned in terms of narrative technique as well as thematic focus. Just as Maigret's geographical range seemingly echoes that of Simenon, so the form of the novels has something of the discipline of the work in progress, which typically involved a highly intensive exercise lasting a month or less.[9] The story itself is usually related by an external, third-person observer who is occasionally able to tap into Maigret's thoughts, but more often intersperses sequences of narrative and description with dramatic scenes featuring dialogue or formal interrogation, usually accompanied by carefully detailed body language. Frequently Maigret will be assigned – or assign himself – to a case, and be set up somewhere near the scene of the crime, for example in a hospital in *Le Fou de Bergerac* (*The Madman of Bergerac*, 1932), or a canal-side inn in *La Tête d'un homme* (*A Battle of Nerves*, 1931), where he will abandon his domestic habits and devote all his time and energy to resolving the situation – which can often have its origins in the distant past. The process will, typically, last for a few days or a week (a time span scrupulously indicated, and spread over ten or a dozen chapters) during which his actions will often seem inconsequential, even incomprehensible, before a conclusion – conventional or not – is reached. The narrative itself will then generally close with a perfunctory rundown of life after the investigation.

Another crucial feature is Simenon's crisp, unfussy language, perfected from the early 1920s, after Colette, one of the first editors of his potboilers, advised him that he should at all costs suppress gratuitous literary effects[10] – advice which, he claimed, led him to limit his vocabulary to no more than 2,000 words. The consequent directness and simplicity – typically reinforced by terse, economical paragraphing – were one obvious way to keep faith with his francophone audience, but they also simplified work on the translations, which began to appear at an early stage. Certainly English versions pose relatively few problems beyond the confusing multiplicity of titles for individual texts, whereby, for instance, *The Yellow Dog* can also be *A Face for a Clue*.

More significantly, the style lends itself perfectly to the economical creation of mood. Essentially, Simenon draws his readers into Maigret's universe within a few sentences of any text and holds them there until the end. And beyond the plot and events this is a matter of enabling them to see, hear and breathe in the features of a given ambiance – whether a busy canal on the edge of Paris, such as *L'Ecluse no. 1* (*The Lock at Charenton*, 1933), the rainy Belgian border in *Chez les Flamands* (*The Flemish Shop*, 1932) or a perpetually foggy seaport in *Le Port des brumes* (*Death of a Harbour-Master*, 1932). The effects are all the more telling for being so succinctly deployed – a windswept station platform, or the interior of a battered taxi – at most recurring as a leitmotif in the course of a narrative, like the pervasive smells of spices in the café in *Le Charretier de 'La Providence'* (*The Crime at Lock 14*). *Maigret and The Hundred Gibbets* is particularly rich in this kind of atmospheric detail, both physical ('his voice, echoing in an atmosphere at once too harsh and too empty') and social ('the superintendent barely had the time to glance into the interior and digest this atmosphere of solidly organized existence').[11] In this novel, the ultimate explanation of a succession of past events will not involve a single arrest, but reveals the past complexities of ambition and disillusion among the members of a liégois secret society: in the end, understanding outweighs investigation, and comprehension counts for more than apprehension. An exchange between Maigret and the investigating judge Coméliau in *A Battle of Nerves* neatly sums up the hierarchy of imperatives at work in the superintendent's thinking:

> 'As a policeman and a public servant I am expected to draw logical conclusions from material evidence …'
> 'And as a human being?'
> 'I wait for moral proof.'[12]

A key text: The Yellow Dog

Like many of the early Maigret novels, *The Yellow Dog* is set entirely outside Paris – in and around the small south Breton port of Concarneau, where Simenon and Tigy spent some of the winter of 1930, with their Great Dane, Olaf. Simenon explored the town thoroughly and captured it in a sequence of sombre, moody photographs of the harbour.[13] Other visual qualities, moreover, surface in the text, through the 'luminous clock' in the historic Old Town and the lighting effects on the buildings from the 'glowing paintbrush' of the lighthouse. But beyond the visual – and somewhat atypically – the situation is more historically specific than in many other novels, with references to the First World War (bombing raids, conscription) and to Concarneau's current economic situation (depression in the canning factories, the onion trade with England).

The story is necessarily set in 1930, since then, as in Simenon's text, 7 November was a Friday. The book was written in March 1931, at Guigneville on the Essonne, printed in April, put on sale soon afterwards and made into a film within a year. Everything begins late on a stormy evening by the harbour, with a cinematic scene in which Mostaguen, a local worthy, is mysteriously shot and nearly killed, near the waterfront. After Maigret is drafted in, Goyard/Servières, one of the regular clients of the Admiral Hotel, disappears, and another, Le Pommeret, dies from strychnine poisoning. Maigret arrests the remaining member of their little coterie, Dr Michoux, apparently for his own protection, amidst growing fear among the mass of local residents and particularly the mayor. Eventually Maigret disentangles a complicated skein of events going back several years to the mid-1920s, and involving Goyard/Servières, Le Pommeret and Michoux as conspirators exploiting and betraying a local sailor: the giant Léon Le Guérec, who has dreamed of a fulfilling future with his fiancée, the waitress Emma.

As elsewhere in the first cycle, Simenon is conscious of bordering on different idioms and uses guiding labels such as 'tragicomedy' (for the shooting of Mostaguen), or 'nightmare' (for the ongoing crisis). Moreover, the range of this kind of reference extends explicitly into contemporary media, as when Maigret finds himself comparing the build-up of panic in the town with the hackneyed device of a sudden, violent storm in a cinema film. Strikingly, a whole crucial sequence, set when Le Guérec rediscovers Emma after their years of separation, is viewed by Maigret and Leroy through a window 'like a film, a silent film without music' (p. 76).[14] More typically, the wind, rain, mud and dark nights dictate the prevailing atmosphere in autumnal Concarneau, and the murky, greenish windowpanes of the Admiral Hotel suggest a note of distortion and mystery. Other motifs do more to intensify the current situation. The enigmatic dog of the original title, who first appears when Mostaguen is shot at, serves initially as a ready focus for all the uncertainties of the frightened townspeople, before his further significance – as Le Guérec's faithful companion and proxy – is eventually revealed. And the 'face for a clue' – that of Emma at the Admiral Hotel: 'a face with no particular grace, yet so appealing that throughout the conversation that followed he hardly stopped watching it. Whenever he turned away, moreover, the waitress, in turn, fixed her gaze on him' (p. 7) yields a similar effect.[15] As Maigret explains when the mystery is finally disentangled: 'When I first got here, I came across one face that appealed to me, and I never let go of it' (p. 99).[16]

The plot of the coterie at the Admiral Hotel – and their involvement with Le Guérec and Emma – is firmly set within the social context of a small provincial community. And beyond – or behind – the recurrent weather features, the historic detail of the streets and houses, and the traditional dress of the locals, is a small town where the apparently well-to-do exploit the less fortunate, where petty social distinctions loom all too large, and where the future seems to depend on dubious property speculation along the coast: where houses lie empty or unfinished, and where, in Dr Michoux's words, there is 'something not quite solid' (p. 64).[17] It is therefore not surprising that, when the chain of menacing events is set off, fear spreads rapidly amongst the anonymous, alienated population out in the streets (chapter 3 is entitled 'Fear reigns in Concarneau'), and that this gives rise to further violence, with the ugly persecution of the innocent yellow dog. At this point the dog becomes a symbol of exclusion (including the exclusion of Le Guérec, his owner) and the principal victim of the prejudice and fear rife in Concarneau, since he will die of the wounds inflicted on him. Later, indeed, Maigret will go so far as to say that fear is what underlies the whole affair. But the fear is not entirely spontaneous either. 'Fear reigns in Concarneau' is in fact the front-page headline of the *Brest Beacon* on Sunday 9 November, and the product of what might be called an elaborate 'press-procedural', with its own commercial agenda, animated by a frantic band of garishly dressed Parisian journalists and photographers installed in the Admiral Hotel, and running parallel to Maigret's own investigation.

After his arrival, Maigret spends three days apparently making negligible progress, but relishing the generalized confusion proliferating around him, before an inspection of Emma's room gives him the facts necessary to convene all the interested parties for a theatrical finale in the police barracks. Dr Michoux is, of course, already there; his overbearing mother has just returned from Paris; Goyard/Servières, who had in fact faked his own disappearance, is brought in by two police inspectors; the 'vagrant', Le Guérec, and Emma, have been intercepted before being able to escape by train; and the mayor of Concarneau represents the anxious crowd outside. Le Guérec explains how in the last few days, having finally returned from his years of imprisonment in New York, he has sought to take his revenge on the sordid little Concarneau coterie, who had set him up, on the maiden voyage of his ship the *Pretty Emma*, with a cargo of cocaine, and thereafter betrayed him to the American authorities, thus consigning him to an open-ended term in Sing Sing prison. (The 1920s 'bootleg' element here can be seen as a further residue of Simenon's pulp output.) Then Maigret sums up events after his own arrival, stressing the utter terror afflicting Michoux, Goyard/Servières and Le Pommeret, but also Léon and Emma's 'silent movie' reconciliation of the previous night, and their willingness to leave everything here behind.

The last few pages have Michoux condemned to twenty years on Devil's Island for the murder of Le Pommeret, Léon Le Guérec fishing for herring in the North Sea, and Emma – now his wife – expecting a child. But, as usual, the final details matter far less than the process leading up to them. In the course of the explanations in the barracks, Maigret has apologized to the mayor for his initial secrecy: 'When I arrived here, I felt quite sure the drama had just begun ... To figure out its pattern, I had to let it develop, heading off further damage as best I could' (pp. 126–7).[18] But earlier, when the superintendent has started to take him into his confidence, the mayor admits: 'You've made me understand the terrible mystery of this business. It's more complex than I ever expected' (p. 92).[19] And earlier still the cowardly and corrupt Dr Michoux has told him: 'I've been watching you. You look like a man who can understand' (p.64).[20] Not, of course, that Maigret's understanding will do other than confirm Michoux's guilt. For the pattern of this drama will, precisely, be that of bourgeois dishonesty and greed set against the honest efforts of the ordinary, deserving people who merit Simenon's sympathy. In a similar vein, Simenon's ability to look beyond restrictive borderlines helps to define his own special contribution to crime fiction. Maigret's walk through Concarneau's historic walls to rescue the yellow dog can surely take on an emblematic value: 'Maigret crossed the drawbridge, passed through the Old Town ramparts, and turned down a crooked, poorly lit street ... As the superintendent advanced ... he entered a zone of ever more ambiguous silence' (p. 38).[21] As this chapter has shown, by its literary trajectory, crossing lines and challenging the borders between mainstream and popular literature, just as much as by its extraordinary statistics, 'the Simenon case' gave a whole new quality and dimension to crime fiction – and not just in the French tradition, but worldwide. There has been no one else remotely like him.

* * *

Extract from Georges Simenon's *The Yellow Dog*

The following extract from The Yellow Dog, *set in the Admiral Hotel, near the waterfront in Concarneau, captures the mood of uncertainty enveloping the town as a whole – and all but one of the characters – just before the serious revelations begin, with the reunion of Le Guérec and Emma, observed, unbeknown to them, by Maigret and Leroy. More particularly, it illustrates various aspects of Simenon's technique: the creation of a dramatic scene, confined to a single room and structured by entrances and exits, dialogue and body language; the building up of suspense, as Maigret tantalizes his listeners – and readers; and the frustrating of expectations as he unexpectedly disappears, removing his commanding presence and so precluding – for a time at least – any possibility of final explanation.*

The effect was the same as when the teacher enters a class-room where the students are chattering. Conversation stopped. The reporters rushed up to the superintendent.

'Can we report the doctor's arrest? Has he confessed?'

'Not at all!'

Maigret waved them aside and called to Emma, 'Two Pernods, my dear.'

'But look, if you've arrested Michoux –'

'You want to know the truth?'

They already had their notebooks in hand. They waited, pens at the ready.

'Well then, there is no truth yet. Maybe there will be some day. Maybe not.'

'We hear that Jean Goyard –'

'Is alive. So much the better for him.'

'But still, there's a man in hiding, and they can't find him.'

'Which goes to prove the hunter's not as smart as the prey.'

Taking Emma by the sleeve, Maigret said gently, 'I'll have my lunch in my room.'

He drank his aperitif down straight and got to his feet.

'A piece of advice, gentlemen! No jumping to conclusions. And no deductions, above all.'

'What about the criminal?'

He shrugged his broad shoulders and murmured: 'Who knows?'

He was already at the foot of the stairs. Inspector Leroy threw him a questioning look.

'No, my friend. You eat down here. I need a rest.'

He climbed the stairs with a heavy tread. Ten minutes later, Emma went up after him with a plate of hors d'œuvres.

Then she carried up a coquille St Jacques and roast veal with spinach.

In the dining-room, conversation languished. One of the reporters was called to the phone.

'Around four o'clock, yes,' he declared. 'I hope to have something sensational for you … Not yet! We've got to wait …

All alone at a table, Leroy ate with the manners of a well-bred boy, regularly wiping his lips with the corner of his napkin.

People outside kept an eye on the Admiral café, hoping vaguely for something to happen.

A policeman leaned against the building at the end of the alleyway where the vagrant had disappeared.

'The mayor is on the phone, asking for superintendent Maigret,' Emma announced.

Leroy jumped. 'Go up and tell him,' he said to her.

The waitress left, but came right back and said, 'He's not there!'

The inspector bounded up the stairs, returned very pale, and snatched the receiver.

'Hello! …Yes, Monsieur le Maire … I don't know. I … I'm very worried … The superintendent has gone … Hello! … No! That's all I can tell you … He had lunch in his room. I didn't see him come down … I … I'll phone you back shortly …'

And Leroy, who had not put his napkin down, used it now to wipe his brow.

Georges Simenon, *The Yellow Dog* (1931), trans. Linda Asher (Harmondsworth: Penguin Books, 2003), pp. 70–1

Notes

1 Early reviewers included Robert Brasillach and André Thérive; Narcejac's book, *Le Cas Simenon*, was first published in 1950; and recent interpretations, from the 1980s onwards, are to be found, for instance, in *Traces* and *Cahiers Simenon*.

2 '*Pietr-le-Letton* n'était pas un chef d'œuvre. Il n'en a pas moins marqué dans ma vie une sorte de charnière.' Quoted in Pierre Assouline, *Simenon*, édition revue et augmentée (Paris: Folio, 1996), p. 195.

3 'En face de l'insularité de la clôture et de l'hyperrationalité du Roman-problème, la série des *Maigret* semble marquer un renversement de la tendance … Avec Maigret, le Roman Policier s'oxygène' (In contrast to the insularity of closure and the hyperrationality of the classic mystery novel, the Maigret series seems to mark a striking reversal … With Maigret, the detective novel gets some fresh air), Jean Fabre, *Enquête sur un enquêteur: Maigret. Un essai de sociocritique* (Montpellier: Études Sociocritiques, 1981), p. 27.

4 'Il n'y a pas de romans … policiers. Et il n'y a pas de règles du genre' (There are no detective novels. And there are no rules for the genre), *Pour Vous*, 15 September 1932.

5 On the abandoning of Maigret, see Georges Simenon, André Gide, *Sans trop de pudeur: correspondance 1938–1950* (Paris: Omnibus, 1999), p. 31; on Simenon as 'our greatest novelist', see ibid., p. 8.

6 'Comme … les différentes intrigues, en raison de traits récurrents, se super-posent aisément, on est induit à tenir les dix-neuf romans pour un seul et grand Texte' (As … the different plots are easily superimposed on each other, due to their recurrent patterns, it is tempting to see the first nineteen novels as a single great Text), Jacques Dubois, *Le Roman policier ou la modernité* (Paris: Nathan, 1992), p. 173

7 'Je ne comprends pas encore tout à fait vos méthodes, commissaire, mais je crois que je commence à deviner' … 'Vous avez de la chance, vieux! Surtout en ce qui concerne cette affaire, dans laquelle ma méthode a été justement de ne pas en avoir …', Georges Simenon, *The Yellow Dog*, trans. Linda Asher, with an introduction by Richard Vinen (Harmondsworth: Penguin Books, 2003), p. 99. All further English quotations and references are to this edition. The other standard translation, *A Face for a Clue*, by Geoffrey Sainsbury, first appeared in 1939.

8 For more detail, see Dubois, *Le Roman policier ou la modernité*, pp. 177–83.

9 See Jacques Dubois and Benoît Denis, 'Introduction', in Simenon, *Romans, I* (Paris: Gallimard, 2003), pp. ix–lxxi (pp. xiv–xxi).

10 See, for instance, Patrick Marnham, *The Man Who Wasn't Maigret: A Portrait of Georges Simenon* (San Diego, New York, London: Harvest, 1992), pp. 141–2.

11 'Sa voix, qui tomba dans une atmosphère trop crue, trop vide'; 'Le commissaire n'eut que le temps d'un regard pour s'imprégner de cette atmosphère d'existence solidement organisée'. Simenon, *Le Pendu de St Pholien*, in *Tout Simenon, 16* (Paris: Omnibus, 2003), pp. 166 and 131.

12 — En tant que fonctionnaire de la police, je suis tenu de tirer des conclusions logiques de preuves matérielles …
— Et en tant qu'homme?
— J'attends les preuves morales.
Simenon, *La Tête d'un homme*, in *Tout Simenon, 16*, p. 748.

13 See *L'Œil de Simenon* (Paris: Éditions du Jeu de Paume, 2004), pp. 97–107.

14 '[T]oujours comme du cinema: du cinéma sans musique', Simenon, *Le Chien Jaune, Tout Simenon*, 16, p. 326.

15 '[U]n visage sans grace et pourtant si attachant que pendant la conversation qui suivit il ne cessa de l'observer. Chaque fois qu'il détourna la tête, d'ailleurs, c'était la fille de salle qui rivait sur lui son regard fièvreux', ibid., p. 281.

16 'Quand je suis arrivé ici, je suis tombé sur une tête qui m'a séduit et je ne l'ai plus lâchée', ibid., p. 342.

17 '[Q]uelque chose de peu solide', ibid., p. 318.

18 'Quand je suis arrivé, j'ai eu la certitude que le drame ne faisait que commencer… Pour en connaître les ficelles, il fallait lui permettre de se développer en évitant autant que possible les dégâts', ibid., p. 359.

19 'Vous m'avez fait toucher du doigt le mystère angoissant, d'une complexité que je ne soupçonnais pas', ibid., p. 337.

[20] 'Je vous ai observé. J'ai l'impression que vous êtes capable de comprendre', ibid., p. 318.

[21] 'Maigret traversa le pont-levis, franchit la ligne des ramparts, s'engagea dans une rue mal éclairée ... Alors que le commissaire avançait, il pénétrait dans une zone de silence de plus en plus équivoque', ibid., p. 301.

Select bibliography and further secondary reading

The novels and short stories appearing in French under Simenon's name between 1931 and 1972 are collected in the twenty-five-volume collection *Tout Simenon*, published by Omnibus, in Paris. Most of these works, and nearly all the Maigret stories, are, or have been available in English, mostly published by Penguin. Two volumes of Simenon, *Romans,* complete with detailed critical apparatus, were published by Gallimard in the Bibliothèque de la Pléiade series in 2003.

There is a huge and ever expanding volume of material on Simenon and Maigret. The following items make up a tiny selection of central items normally available to the English-language reader:

Assouline, Pierre, *Simenon* (Paris: Folio, 1996).

——, *Simenon: A Biography* (London: Chatto and Windus, 1997).

Becker, Lucille, *Georges Simenon Revisited* (New York: Twayne, 1999).

——, *Georges Simenon: Maigret and the 'Romans Durs'* (London: H Books, 2006).

Boyer, Régis, *'Le Chien jaune' de Georges Simenon* (Paris: Hachette, 1973).

Eskin, Stanley, *Simenon: A Critical Biography* (Jefferson and London: McFarland, 1987).

Fabre, Jean, *Enquête sur un enquêteur. Maigret: un essai de sociocritique* (Montpellier: Études Sociocritiques, 1981).

Lemoine, Michel, *L'Autre Univers de Simenon* (Liège: CLPCF, 1991).

——, *Simenon: écrire l'homme* (Paris: Gallimard, 2003).

Marnham, Patrick, *The Man Who Wasn't Maigret: A Portrait of Georges Simenon* (London: Bloomsbury, 1992).

Narcejac, Thomas, *Le Cas Simenon* (Paris: Presses de la Cité, 1950).

Piron, Maurice, with Michel Lemoine, *L'Univers de Simenon. Guide des romans et nouvelles (1931–1972) de Georges Simenon* (Paris: Presses de la Cité, 1983).

Vanoncini, André, *Simenon et l'affaire Maigret* (Paris: Honoré Champion, 1990).

Periodicals and study centres

Cahiers Simenon (Brussels: Les Amis de Georges Simenon).

Traces (Liège: Centre d'Études Georges Simenon, Université de Liège).

There is also a Simenon Center at Drew University, Madison, New Jersey.

Websites

Websites, too, continue to develop rapidly. The following are authoritative, and provide links to other sources:

http://www.libnet.ulg.ac.be/simenon/biogrsim.htm
http://www.toutsimenon.com/Mem/menu1.htm
http://www.trussell.com

3

Post-War French Crime Fiction: the Advent of the Roman Noir

CLAIRE GORRARA

The late 1940s and 1950s witnessed an explosion of crime writing in France. After the enforced deprivation of all things American under German occupation, the gritty thrillers of the hard-boiled school of writing came to epitomize the mixture of fascination and repulsion with which France greeted a tidal wave of American capital and culture. Translations of American and British authors, such as Dashiell Hammett, Raymond Chandler, James Hadley Chase and Peter Cheyney, initially swelled the ranks of crime fiction series launched to meet the demand for American popular culture. However, French authors were soon drawn to adopt what became known as the *roman noir* in deference to the black and white covers of the Série Noire, Gallimard's premier crime fiction collection created in 1945. Whilst a fair proportion of these early French *romans noirs* can be considered as little more than a pale imitation or pastiche of their American and British counterparts, this is far from the whole story. For it was during the late 1940s and the 1950s that a small group of French writers appropriated the *roman noir* as a privileged vehicle for examining post-war France, depicting a nation grappling with the traumatic legacy of the recent past and overwhelmed by the unprecedented pace of economic and social modernization.

This chapter will begin by setting out the social, political and economic context for the emergence of the *roman noir* in immediate post-war France and its relationship to broader trends in the production of post-war popular culture. It will then examine the ambivalent reception accorded American and British hard-boiled crime fiction and outline the narrative template such fiction offered French writers. By exploring selected novels by a group of four writers, André Héléna, Jean Amila, Terry Stewart and Léo Malet, the chapter will discuss the ways in which the French *roman noir* has, from its inception, functioned as a form of social investigation, a disabused narrative of its times, often narrated from the perspective of the dispossessed, excluded and marginalized. The novels of these writers will be analysed as 'voices from the margins', texts that provide an alternate history of post-war reconstruction saturated in a *noir* aesthetic; for such writers laid the foundations for a tradition of critically engaged crime writing that continues to shape the form and function of crime fiction in France today.

War, culture and reconstruction

France of the late 1940s was a country struggling to recover from the experiences of the Second World War. During May and June 1940, French forces suffered the ignominy of defeat in just four weeks when faced with the combined air and ground assault of German troops. With the collapse of the Third Republic, the power vacuum was filled by the collaborationist Vichy regime, headed by the octogenarian Marshall Pétain, a veteran military leader from the First World War, who was initially regarded as the saviour of the French people. Yet, even as the armistice was signed, it became clear that the cessation of hostilities was but the beginning of a period of hardship, deprivation and increasing political and social repression, *les années noires* or dark years of occupation. France was divided into a number of zones, curtailing basic freedom of movement and leaving large swathes of the country under German control. France's industrial infrastructure was put at the service of the German war economy, whilst essential goods and supplies were rationed and profiteering worsened the already bleak outlook for ordinary French men and women. In terms of the human costs of occupation, over 1.7 million French men were expelled from France, whether as prisoners of war, conscripted workers or political and racial deportees. Indeed, French state collusion in the persecution and deportation of Jews living in France would come to stand as one of the most shameful memories of this period. With the Liberation, the undeclared war between those who had supported the Nazis and the Vichy regime and those who were involved in the French resistance in its myriad forms erupted into all-out civil war. This took the form of summary trials and executions, the public head-shaving of women who were accused of collaboration and the purging of public administration, industry and other influential arenas of public life. These activities, some sanctioned by the newly formed political elites, some more nebulously located on the borders between legality and illegality, came to represent the desire to start afresh, to wipe the slate clean, as France took up its place in a new world order.

The task of reconstruction was a monumental one. Not only was France a country devastated by the ravages of war, it was also a nation conscious of the need to reassert itself on the world stage after the humiliations of defeat and occupation. The post-war elites in France were, therefore, faced with the need not only to reconstruct the political institutions and economic infrastructure of the nation but also to engage in a cultural rebirth that would signal France's national identity as a forward-looking and modernizing society. In politics, the successful coalition of socialists, democrats and communists during the early years of the Fourth Republic gave hope for a reconfiguration of party politics, based on cooperation and consensus rather than divisive sectarianism. In the economic sphere, new models of industrial planning and the decisive role played by American investment in the form of the Marshall Plan yielded fruit in the phenomenal productivity levels of the 1950s, setting France on the path towards *les trente glorieuses* (the thirty glorious years), its boom years of expansion and growth from 1944 to 1974. At the same time the cultural supremacy of France seemed assured by the growing reputation of French intellectuals and writers, such as Jean-Paul Sartre, Simone de Beauvoir and Albert Camus, whose existential novels, plays and essays chimed with the muted optimism of the immediate post-war years.

The rewards of such rapid modernization were, however, little in evidence in the late 1940s as inflation, continued rationing, unemployment, labour strikes, shortage of social housing and a series of harsh winters led many French men and women to speculate that the prosperity promised by government leaders had failed to materialize. To this was added the distant echo of colonial conflicts as France's determination to retain its overseas territories was challenged by nationalist movements, most notably in Indochina (1946–54) where a fragile negotiated settlement erupted into full-scale war. By the late 1950s, the spectre of war in Algeria, the jewel in the crown of the French empire, divided the nation and set France on a path that would ultimately lead to Algerian independence and the fall of the Fourth Republic, fatally undermined by its failure to decolonize. Yet whilst this dark history would reverberate throughout the decade, the 1950s were also years that witnessed the coming of an American-identified consumer culture.[1] The growing prosperity that had been largely confined to the middle classes in the immediate aftermath of war trickled down into working-class homes with dramatic effects. From cars, fridges, washing machines and television, to Formica and fashion magazines, a whole host of products transformed French life. A new generation of French consumers sprang into existence who had both the leisure time and the disposable income to devote to acquiring such markers of modernity and the cultural values they embodied.

One of the arenas of French life that benefited from the successes of economic modernization and the rise of a consumer society was popular culture. Cinema attendance reached new heights in the late 1940s.[2] Both American imports and indigenous production catered for a voracious public appetite for genres as diverse as classic literary adaptations and the haunting cityscape of American *film noir*, a cinematographic style that captured the imagination of French critics and film makers alike. In publishing, the launch of the Livre de Poche venture in 1953 inaugurated a paperback revolution that brought literature to the people in an accessible and affordable format. Radio, well established before and during the war years, became a primary outlet for a new generation of French singers, fashioned by the global dominance of American rock and roll, and television gradually became a feature of French homes into the 1960s. In the world of journalism, the creation of mass-circulation weekly magazines, such as *Elle*, *L'Express* and *Paris-Match*, competed against rival American publications for market share. Yet, whilst American models provided inspiration and helped shape the profile of French popular culture, they also drew negative assessments. For if the ruling elites demonstrated ambivalence towards American investment in French industry – soliciting aid but fearful of its impact on French working practices – similar attitudes were discernable in the cultural sphere and nowhere more so than in relation to the *roman noir*.

The emergence of the roman noir

American hard-boiled crime fiction was one of the publishing sensations of the late 1940s. Exported en masse to France in the post-war era, crime fiction collections, such as the Série Noire, published American and British novels in translation that had little or no cultural legitimacy in their country of origin. Collected together under the banner of the *roman noir*, they acquired a group identity and cultural cachet that generated enormous interest not only in France but across Europe as other countries began to recognize the originality of such a body of writing. However, these critical considerations were far from the mind of the first editor of the Série Noire, Marcel Duhamel, whose *noir* manifesto, as printed on the book jackets of the early novels in the series, provides a humorous insight into early reader responses to this dynamic form of crime fiction:

The unsuspecting reader should beware: volumes of the Série noire cannot be safely given to all. The amateur reader of Sherlock Holmes-style mysteries will like little about them, neither will the general optimist ... Their tone is rarely conformist. They present policemen who are more corrupt than the thieves they pursue. The friendly detective does not always solve the mystery. Sometimes there is no mystery and sometimes no detective at all... But what remain are action, anguish and violence, in all their most execrable forms – particularly brutal beatings and killings. Like all good films, the inner workings of the mind are translated into actions and readers who are fond of introspective literature will have to perform a sort of reverse mental gymnastics ... tumultuous passion, unforgiving hatred, all emotions that, in a closely policed society, are only meant to be exceptional occurrences are here quite run of the mill and sometimes expressed in a less than scholarly language ...[3]

Duhamel clearly situates the early *roman noir* as the direct antithesis of the murder-mystery novel that had dominated the interwar years in France. The rarefied social settings, clearly defined character types and reliance upon an omniscient detective able to restore social harmony have no place in these disturbing narratives. Chaos and violence determine social relations rather than reason and logic. Duhamel deliberately highlights the challenge such novels pose to conventional morality as the institutions of law and order are found to be either systematically corrupt or incompetent and the reader cannot retain the comforting illusion of criminals being called to account and good triumphing over evil. Instead, Duhamel revels in the thrills and spills of these *romans noirs* and promotes the vicarious enjoyment of the reader, immersed in a world awash with graphic accounts of murder and sex.

Yet, if Duhamel presents these early *romans noirs* as overturning the formal conventions of traditional detective fiction, he also acknowledges the revolutionary impact they would have on the aesthetics of crime writing. By comparing the *roman noir* to film, Duhamel emphasizes the visual quality of such writing, its cinematographic appeal, as imagery, action and dialogue predominate over psychological introspection. One of the defining features of the post-war decades would be the cross-fertilization of fiction and film as French film directors and *roman noir* novelists collaborated on adaptations that would see a good number of these early novels brought to the screen.[4] Indeed, this focus on emotion and action would play a significant role in the development of a style and tone for the French *roman noir*. A colourful 'street' language or *argot* became the hallmark of an important grouping of French crime novels in these early years epitomized by the work of writers like Albert Simonin,

Auguste Le Breton and José Giovanni. The stylized vernacular of novels, such as Simonin's *Touchez pas au grisbi!* (1953) was credited with bringing a specifically French pace and rhythm to the depiction of a post-war criminal underworld and spawned a whole cottage industry in dictionaries of slang to accompany the novels.

Duhamel's promotion of the early novels published in the Série Noire also highlights many of the issues that made the *roman noir* such a controversial narrative form in France. Whilst many readers were attracted to its repudiation of bourgeois conventions and sensibilities and its formal innovation, others regarded the deluge of Americanized fiction as an assault on French traditions and cultural values. For critic and detective fiction writer Thomas Narcejac, the *roman noir américain* was little more than sensationalist and voyeuristic mass culture, appealing to readers' baser instincts. It had no affinities with 'noble' traditions of detective writing that engaged the reader in an intellectual battle of wits with the author. Indeed, its arrival promised to reduce a lively indigenous culture of detective novels to mere formulaic fiction as French authors attempted to exploit the vogue for excessive violence and sexual titillation.[5] Others, such as André Piljean, himself a Série Noire writer, went further, fearing that French authors would lose their publishing outlets and warning of an American *plan d'invasion*, conjuring up troubling images of a cultural colonization that tapped into French anxieties as a country newly liberated from occupation.[6]

Certainly, the fears expressed by Narcejac and Piljean had some justification. Of the first one hundred titles in the Série Noire, only five were penned by French or French-speaking authors. Of these, Belgian Yvan Dailly's *J'ai bien l'honneur* (1951) is symptomatic of a large percentage of French-authored *romans noirs* of the 1950s in being little more than a slavish imitation of the American masters. In a plot centred on two former GIs and their bungled heist of a pharmacy, the novel replicates many of the more hackneyed clichés of American hard-boiled crime fiction, from 'honour amongst thieves' to the highly sexualized portrayal of the femme fatale. Yet, these now dated reproductions of an American model should not hide what was to become the major development of these years in France. Alongside such crass exploitation, a corpus of writing was to emerge that adapted the American hard-boiled crime novel to suit contemporary French concerns and anxieties.

During the late 1940s and 1950s, a small number of French writers were instrumental in creating a vocation and mission for the post-war *roman noir* as an impassioned social history of the present and the recent past. Writers such as Jean Amila, Terry Stewart, André Héléna and Léo

Malet experimented with form and content, in some cases producing novels that adopted an American perspective and voice but, increasingly, they were drawn to targeting directly France's own chequered history of war, occupation and reconstruction. What united such writers was the urgent need to expose social injustices and the political and economic collusions that fuelled post-war reconstruction across the Western world. These novelists catalogue the disastrous consequences of rampant capitalism; they tackle contentious topics, such as the continuing use of the death penalty,[7] and they contest the authority and legitimacy of the ruling political elites. Yet, this combative tone does not mean that their novels read today as little more than pamphlets or left-wing propaganda. The *noir* aesthetic that made American authors, such as Dashiell Hammett and Raymond Chandler, so admired in some circles informs the writing of these novelists and their use of sophisticated literary strategies. Often narrated from the perspective of those most vulnerable to displacement and exclusion, many of these early novels confound reader expectations by their creation of unreliable first-person narrators whose accounts challenge our assumptions about narrative coherence and order. It is this fusion of form and function that would make these early French *romans noirs* such pioneering fiction for subsequent generations of writers.

Voices from the margins

The writing careers of Jean Amila, Terry Stewart, André Héléna and Léo Malet are indicative of the conditions under which many French authors of the late 1940s and 1950s laboured to produce crime fiction. All wrote using a number of pseudonyms, indeed, Amila and Stewart were themselves pseudonyms under which these two authors become widely known, and they migrated between different crime fiction collections as they strove to place their work.[8] None of these authors entertained literary pretensions of grandeur and they saw themselves primarily as artisans or workers whose prolific production was a way to earn money. Whilst their novels suggest that all, at some point, had left-wing sympathies, they rejected institutional politics in one form or another, preferring the role of maverick commentator. Yet their early novels present a highly critical vision of post-war reconstruction, seen either through the lens of an American camera or more directly focused on French realities.

The first two French writers to be published in the Série Noire were promoted and marketed as American in order to capitalize on the vogue for American hard-boiled crime fiction. Jean Amila and Terry Stewart masked the identities of Jean Meckert and Serge Arcouët respectively, both of whom would set their first Série Noire novels in a mythical America that threw back distorted reflections of a post-war France in crisis. Meckert was a writer of considerable talent who had already published five novels under his real name to critical acclaim before he embarked on a 'second' career and identity as a Série Noire writer.[9] Fêted by the literary establishment of the day as a lyrical chronicler of the hardships of working-class life, Meckert's highly politicized vision of the violent contradictions between individual aspiration and repressive social structures and institutions would find a fitting outlet in the Série Noire under the pseudonyms of John, then Jean, Amila.[10]

Y a pas de bon dieu! (1950), Amila's first foray into the Série Noire, recounts the story of Pastor Paul Wiseman, a Methodist preacher and spokesperson for the small community of Mowalla threatened with extinction by the building of a dam that would flood their valley and obliterate their village. The combined forces of big business and the local law enforcement agencies conspire to discredit their campaign (claiming that they are communist rebel rousers), whilst in fact preparing for a far more devastating exploitation of the land for uranium extraction. Narrated from the perspective of Pastor Wiseman, the main protagonist's gradual descent into violence and amoral behaviour is charted with sympathy and resignation as he conducts a compromising affair with a young girl and replicates the violent tactics of his opponents by beating senseless an opponent. The 'wise man', meant like Moses to lead his people to safety, is shown to lose the moral high ground and to employ the same inhuman tactics as his adversaries. Based on the real-life story of the French village of Tignes, flooded to make way for a dam project, the narrative highlights many of the fears surrounding the impact of American investment on immediate post-war French society: its corrosive influence on moral and cultural values; the destruction of communities as American commercial imperatives disregard local traditions and customs and the sense that institutions meant to offer support and succour, such as the Church, are complicit in the reduction of ordinary people's lives and aspirations to profit margins and spreadsheets.[11]

Terry Stewart's *La Belle Vie* takes an equally jaundiced view of the human costs of modernization, this time in a novel narrated from the perspective of a union leader, Mears Conway, during a strike at a refrigeration plant in the industrial heartland of America. Here, a cast of heroic losers demonstrates the extent to which individual tragedy is attributable not only to inner demons but also to the workings of unrestrained

American-style capitalism. Mears Conway exhibits many of the same tendencies as Amila's Pastor Wiseman as a man meant to lead a 'chosen' people to the promised land of prosperity and opportunity but who gives into temptation. As in Amila's novel, business interests and the forces of law and order orchestrate confrontations that lead to the deaths of loved ones and confirm the futility of campaigning for better working conditions when self-interest and greed shatter working-class solidarity. Published in 1950, the novel exposes the exploitation of the workers in the name of economic efficiency in ways that would resonate with French post-war reconstruction. For the first readers of *La Belle Vie* could not have failed to make the connection between the doomed strike action of the novel and the wave of industrial unrest that engulfed France in 1947–8 as communist-backed strikes threatened to derail post-war reconstruction and were ruthlessly quashed by the forces of law and order. As with Amila's *Y a pas de bon dieu!*, the main protagonist fails in his battle against far more powerful vested interests, leading to the decimation of the community he represents and the victory of global capitalism.

If these two early *romans noirs* situated in an imagined America offered their first French readers the comforting illusion that violence and civil unrest could be safely cordoned off in foreign lands, other French *romans noirs* of the period were far less easily dismissed. Jean Amila/Meckert, in addition to his 'Americanized' novels, also published highly incendiary crime narratives grounded in French historical realities.[12] For, increasingly, over the immediate post-war decades, selected French crime writers turned to the *roman noir* as a means of exposing the hypocrisies and empty promises of those in power in France, giving such a popular literary form an explosive political charge. One such writer was André Héléna who began his crime writing career in 1949 with *Les Flics ont toujours raison!*, an impassioned denunciation of the inequalities and brutality of the French penal system. Héléna went on to write thirty-seven *romans noirs* of uneven quality, as well as *romans érotiques* and a number of film screenplays. Now the subject of literary studies and critical reappraisals, Héléna's growing reputation is largely predicated on his crime fiction set during the German occupation of France and published in the late 1940s and 1950s. Such novels have been justly credited with challenging reader expectations and assumptions of heroic resistance and venal collaboration in favour of far more complex realities that depict the moral uncertainties of life under German occupation.[13]

Les Salauds ont la vie dure! (1949) scandalized the French authorities when it was published in the years following France's bloody liberation.

Condemned as an affront to public decency, it was banned from publication in 1953 and the film of the novel, already in production, was axed due to government pressure.[14] What made this novel and its sequel, *Le Festival des macchabées* (1951), so shocking to the authorities was Héléna's deliberate demystification of France's war record and the emphasis on the betrayals, subterfuges and pervasive corruption of *les années noires*. Narrated from the perspective of Maurice Delbar, a petty crook and black marketeer, the novel takes the reader on a picaresque journey through occupied France: from the twilight world of Parisian gangsterism to collaborationist milieux and resistance groups in Lyon before ending in the mountains of the Pyrenees as Maurice throws in his lot with local resistance fighters.[15] Throughout the novel, Héléna presents the Occupation as a time of internecine conflict as the French militia and resistance groups commit equally heinous crimes. Maurice, recruited as a hired assassin for the local resistance, becomes a symbol of the moral turpitude of the era, animated as he is by greed and self-interest and devoid of any patriotic spirit. A troubling moral equivalence floats over the text, suggesting that no side harboured any illusions about the 'criminal' actions that were required to further their cause. Easy loyalties and opportunism characterize Héléna's depiction of a nation at war with itself.

If *Les Salauds ont la vie dure!* represents the Occupation as a time of criminal intentions, acts and agents, Héléna's later novel, *Les Clients du Central Hôtel* (1959), casts the war years in a very different light, privileging a history of victimhood. Set during the heady days of armed insurrection at the Liberation, *Les Clients du Central Hôtel* does away with the narrative focus on a single anti-hero, such as Maurice, and is structured instead around the lives of a number of characters who are brought together by chance as guests at the Central Hotel in Perpignan. The splintered narrative and multiple stories highlight the diversity of experiences during the Occupation as the city is engulfed in violence and factionalism. English secret agents, black-market dealers, prostitutes and informers rub shoulders with Jews in hiding, naive young resisters and the wife of a French prisoner of war in an image of the intersecting destinies of a country where all conventional political and social reference points have broken down. The Central Hotel's proprietor, Mme Poteau, a drug addict and predatory lesbian, appears to symbolize the dulled senses and moral perversions of occupation as atrocities are committed on all sides and individuals are caught up in the adrenalin rush of combat. Yet the black humour and coldly impersonal tone of *Les Salauds ont la vie dure!* is absent in this text. Héléna's sympathies in *Les Clients du Central Hôtel* are far more with the suffering of the French populace as a whole and the traumatic effects of such generalized violence on the individual and the collective. Here, each victim of violence is given a substance and signifi- cance; from the German soldier killed in hand-to-hand combat to the young woman accused of sexual collaboration and raped by three *faux résistants* (fake resisters). Dignity in death is accorded even those who have committed unforgivable crimes, such as the female informant who betrays an English secret agent, in a final image of the extent to which all the characters in the narrative submit to, as well as commit, atrocities and abuses.

The Occupation setting of Héléna's most accomplished work is repre- sentative of the important role the war years themselves would play in the development of the French *roman noir.* They provide the link to perhaps the most influential French *roman noir* writer of the 1940s and 1950s in France, Léo Malet. A surrealist poet with affiliations to pre-war anarch- ism, Malet is often presented as the founding father of the French *roman noir* largely due to the publication of *120, rue de la gare* (1943), consid- ered to be the first authentically French *roman noir*. Set against the backdrop of the Occupation, *120, rue de la gare* introduced French readers to the first private eye in French fiction, Nestor Burma, who, at the beginning of the novel, is languishing in a prisoner-of-war camp in Germany. Once released, he investigates the mysterious death of an am- nesiac fellow prisoner of war and discovers the location of a missing treasure. In so doing, he criss-crosses an occupied France, richly evoca- tive of oppression in terms of *noir* metaphors and motifs as the strict censorship of these years prevented any explicit criticism of the occupier. In *120, rue de la gare*, the familiar *noir* tropes carry added menace as blackouts, rationing and travel restrictions suggest a country in thrall to faceless bureaucrats, able to decide people's destinies at the stroke of a pen, whilst the transitory spaces and places of the *roman noir,* such as bars, hotels and train stations, indicate a sense of displacement and disorienta- tion as characters are uprooted by the experiences of war and consumed by an all-pervasive terror that infects social relations. In *120, rue de la gare*, we are presented with a nation adrift where the only hope for recovery is symbolized by Nestor Burma, an agent of social justice who steps in where the authorities fail.

Burma would be a recurring figure in Malet's *romans noirs*, most famously in a cycle of adventures *Les Nouveaux Mystères de Paris* (1954–9), each set in a different *arrondissement* or district of Paris.[16] Malet's aim in choosing such locations for his crime narratives was to uncover the local histories of Paris as each mystery interacted with its environment in subtly allusive ways. Yet these are novels also shot through with national and transnational histories as France's past comes to haunt the present and the influence of global capital corrupts and destroys former alliances and even identities. This is particularly the case in *Brouillard au pont Tolbiac (Fog on the Tolbiac Bridge*, 1956), set in the thirteenth *arrondissement*, a place of misfortune and ill chance that strikes dread into the heart of Burma.[17]

At the beginning of the novel, Burma is called to the Salpetrière hospital by a strange note from a patient whom, it transpires, he once knew as a young man when he frequented anarchist circles living in the Vegan foyer on rue Tolbiac. In an extended flashback to these days, Burma recreates the anarchist milieux of France during the 1920s and 1930s and speculates on his own 'betrayal' of such youthful ideals. For, like other characters in the novel, he has sold out and become if not an establishment figure then at least one of those who profits from the current regime. Abel Benoît/Albert Lenantais, the hospital patient and victim of crime, is one of the few who has remained faithful to past ideals, living as a rag-and-bone man in a striking image of the excluded of French society, reduced to surviving off the detritus of others. Those who cover up his murder are former anarchist sympathizers, Baurénot and Deslandes, now turned rich timber merchants. They represent the aspirations of the new France but also the immorality and greed from which such wealth springs. Burma, as the figure caught between the two extremes – idealistic renunciation of consumerism or hearty embrace of Western capitalism – walks the streets of the thirteenth *arrondissement* like a lost soul, divided from his past and out of step with the present.

The depiction of the city in *Brouillard au pont Tolbiac* reinforces Malet's vision of a country inexorably caught up in the complex processes of modernization. Paris is at once a symbol of modernity and progress, as transport networks (roads, trains, waterways) all suggest a sense of connection between people and places, a forward momentum. Yet, the Parisian metro as the narrative thread that weaves together all the destinies in the novel, from Burma's first encounter with his gypsy lover, Belita, to the final confrontation between Burma and Baurénot on the viaduct d'Austerlitz, also suggests circularity, repeated return and the possibility that these characters are not in transit but inevitably heading for the terminus. Wreathed in the bewildering fog of the title, it is, however, through Malet's descriptions of the built environment that a *noir* vision of 1950s France is most graphically expressed.[18]

Throughout the novel, the reader is confronted with images of derelict and abandoned houses at night. They come to represent the sense of a nation in terminal decline. This is illustrated clearly in the extract at the end of this chapter. Burma is searching for the final resting place of a bank messenger killed during a robbery some twenty-five years earlier. As he enters the rue Brunesseau, Burma notes the paradoxes of modernization, a sports stadium in the course of construction alongside an expanse of wasteland, new money flooding in for leisure pursuits whilst other more pressing concerns, such as social housing, do not fit the list of government priorities. The house itself, set back from the road, plays to the visual conventions of gothic horror: dogs howling, high winds and the single gnarled tree in the garden, a marker of the lifelessness that permeates the house and the district. As Burma descends into the cellar, he feels like a vampiric intruder, whilst the rather comic image of a corpse in a Salvation Army uniform lessens the shock of discovery with gallows humour. As elsewhere in the novel, these isolated buildings are almost always revealed to be hastily improvised mausoleums, their dead occupants gesturing towards an inverted history of city and nation as the encroachment of the past transforms the bustling metropolis into a ghostly necropolis. As Burma's investigation reaches its close, there are no happy endings, either for the main protagonist or for those whom he encounters on his peripatetic travels through Paris past and present.

In conclusion, the four authors whose work has been studied in this chapter can be considered as pioneers of the *roman noir* in France. They adapted the form and vision of an American-identified model to serve as a searing indictment of France in the late 1940s and 1950s. With their campaigning tone and readiness to intervene in topical debates, they constructed a purpose for the French *roman noir* as a chronicle of its times which instinctively and passionately championed the cause of the oppressed and marginalized. This is achieved largely though a sophisti-cated use of style and tone as a *noir* sensibility colours the depiction of urban landscapes, streaked through with existential metaphors of entrap-ment, circularity and decline. With the exception of Léo Malet, their work has received little sustained critical attention to date but this is changing. Jean Meckert's fiction is currently being reissued by Éditions Joelle Losfeld to critical acclaim.[19] Héléna too has had selected novels repub-lished in the first decade of the twenty-first century and his posthumous rehabilitation was perhaps most clearly signalled by an exhibition of his life and works at the Bibliothèque des littératures policières, Paris, in 2001. After years of relative neglect, these early French *roman noir* writers are now beginning to be read more widely and to be considered justly as the 'missing link' in a genealogy of French crime fiction that stretches back to the nineteenth century and forward to the highly politicized crime fiction of writers such as Jean-Patrick Manchette, Didier Daeninckx and Thierry Jonquet. No longer *des écrivains maudits* (cursed writers), they now stand as worthy of inclusion in the pantheon of great French authors whose work has helped shaped French crime fiction into the twenty-first century.

* * *

Extract from Léo Malet's *Fog on the Tolbiac Bridge*

Nestor Burma has gone to investigate an abandoned house on the rue Brunesseau in the thirteenth arrondissement. A former anarchist and bank robber, Lacorre, has confessed in a letter to killing a young bank messenger, Monsieur Daniel, some twenty-five years previously with two accomplices and burying him in the family home in the cellar. Situated towards the end of the novel, this scene proves climatic in that Lacorre himself is found murdered in the house in a startling reversal of fortune as natural justice appears to have been exacted:

A chain dangled from one of the posts flanking the front gate. The feeble sound it made when I pulled it was swept away by the gale. A dog woke up nearby and started to bark. I rang again. No answer. The dog wasn't barking now. It was howling. The wall wasn't very high. I scrambled over into the garden and made for the house. Its appearance would have put off the toughest squatter. A ramp led down to the cellar. I went down the ramp, came to a door and started to fiddle with the lock. What with the wind shrieking in the leafless branches of a single gnarled old tree, the dog howling, and the musty smell issuing from inside the cellar, I felt like Nosferatu the Vampire. The lock yielded. I stepped forward and lit a match. Right. I still didn't know if there was a stiff underneath the earthen floor, but there was certainly one on top of it. A nice, fresh corpse in a Sally Army uniform. Plugged full of lead. Lacorre, to judge from what I remembered of his ugly mug.

Léo Malet, *Fog on the Tolbiac Bridge* (1956), trans. Barbara Bray (London: Pan Macmillan Publishers Ltd, 1993), p. 130.

Notes

[1]   For a highly influential reading of the entwined histories of decolonization and modernization in France of the 1950s and 1960s, see Kristin Ross's *Fast Cars, Clean Bodies: Decolonization and the Reordering of French Culture* (Cambridge, MA: MIT Press, 1995).

[2] According to film historian Pierre Sorlin, the years 1946–55 were a golden age for French cinema with viewing figures peaking at 430 million in 1947 to settle at 400 million for the rest of the decade. See Pierre Sorlin, 'Transition and social change in the French and Italian cinemas of the reconstruction', in N. Hewitt (ed.), *The Culture of Reconstruction: European Literature, Thought and Film 1945–1950* (London: Macmillan, 1989), p. 89.

[3] 'Que le lecteur non prévenu se méfie: les volumes de la Série noire ne peuvent pas sans danger être mis entre toutes les mains. L'amateur d'enigmes à la Sherlock Holmes n'y trouvera pas son compte. L'optimiste non plus … L'esprit est rarement conformiste. On y voit des policiers plus corrompus que les malfaiteurs qu'ils poursuivent. Le détective sympathique ne résout pas toujours le mystère. Parfois il n'y a pas de mystère. Et quelque fois pas de détective du tout… Alors il reste de l'action, de l'angoissse, de la violence – sous toutes ses formes et particulièrement les plus honnies – du tabassage et du massacre. Comme dans les bons films, les états d'âme se traduisent par des gestes, et les lecteurs friands de littérature introspective devront se livrer à la gymnastique inverse … de la passion désordonnée, de la haine sans merci, tous sentiments qui, dans une société policée, ne sont censés avoir cours que tout à fait exceptionnellement, mais qui sont ici monnaie courante et sont parfois exprimés dans une langue fort peu académique …'

[4] This process of adaptation could also be inverted with films 'novelized' for a new audience, such as André Cayatte's *Nous sommes tous des assassins* (1952), a searing indictment of the horror and inhumanity of the death penalty still in operation in post-war France. Adapted by Jean Meckert and published under the same title in 1952, the novel was promoted by Cayatte and his script writer Charles Spaak as a powerful transposition that retained the campaigning spirit of the original film.

[5] Such a critique is powerfully evinced in Narcejac's *La Fin d'un bluff: essai sur le roman noir américain* (Paris: Le Portulan, 1949).

[6] Quoted in Deborah E. Hamilton, 'The *roman noir* and the reconstruction of national identity in postwar France', in A. Mullen and E. O'Beirne (eds), *Crime Scenes: Detective Narratives in European Culture Since 1945* (Amsterdam: Rodopi, 2000), pp. 228–40 (p. 230).

[7] The psychological terror and torture suffered by the prison inmate on death row lie at the heart of three novels by these authors: Terry Stewart's *La Mort et l'ange* (1948), Jean Meckert's *Nous sommes tous des assassins* (1952) and André Héléna's *Le Condamné à mort* (1959).

[8] Héléna, for example, wrote under nine 'official' pseudonyms for a variety of crime fiction collections. His work also appeared under a further six pseudonyms, re-edited by unscrupulous publishers in pirated versions. See Franck Evrard, *André Héléna, les secrets d'un auteur de romans noirs* (Paris: Bier-Press, 2000), for an exhaustive bibliographical survey of Héléna's fictional production.

[9] For a thought-provoking examination of the literary and political trajectory of Amila's fiction, see David Platten, 'Violence and the saint: political commit-

ment in the fiction of Jean Amila', in David Gascoigne (ed.), *Violent Histories: Violence, Culture and Identity in France from Surrealism to the Néo-Polar* (Oxford/Bern: Peter Lang, 2007), pp. 175–98.

[10] It is widely reported that Meckert chose this name as a contraction of the phrase 'ami l'anar' (the anarchist is your friend) signalling his political sympathies and values.

[11] See Nathaniel Tribondeau, 'La Petite Voix américaine de J. Amila', *813, les amis de la littérature policière*, 93 (2005), 13–19, for an intriguing reading of *Y a pas de bon dieu!* that highlights the interplay of the American 'voice' and French preoccupations of Amila.

[12] See, for example, Jean Meckert, *Nous avons les mains rouges* (1947), a powerful exposé of resistance violence and political dogma set in post-Liberation France.

[13] David Platten's 'Outlaws and miscreants: André Héléna and *les années noires*', forthcoming in his *Outsiders, Radicals and Storytellers: French Crime Fiction in the Modern Era*, offers a detailed investigation of Héléna's wartime novels and their recasting of occupied France via the tropes and motifs of *noir* fiction.

[14] Robert Deleuze, 'Petite histoire du roman noir français', *Les Temps modernes*, 595 (1997), 53–87 (63).

[15] The life and times of Maurice bear a striking resemblance to the real-life figure of Pierre Loutrel, known as Pierrot le fou, whose criminal exploits and dalliance with first collaborationist then resistance milieux was the object of much press speculation and sensation in the late 1940s.

[16] The extraordinary warmth and affection still felt towards Malet's literary creation, Nestor Burma, can be gauged by Patrick Pécherot's critically acclaimed trilogy of novels featuring 'Nestor Burma': *Les Brouillards de la butte* (2001), *Belleville-Barcelone* (2003) and *Boulevard des branques* (2005). Playing upon reader familiarity with the rich cultural intertexts of Malet's work, these 'new' mysteries are both homage to and pastiche of Malet's 1950s crime novels.

[17] For an evocative reading of space, place and cultural memory in *Fog on the Tolbiac Bridge*, sees Teresa Bridgeman, 'Paris-polar in the fog: power of place and generic space in Malet's *Brouillard au pont Tolbiac*', *Australian Journal of French Studies*, 35/1 (1998), 58–74.

[18] The visually arresting nature of Malet's work is evidenced in the successful recasting of a number of his Burma adventures as *bandes dessinées* or graphic novels. Eight of the Burma adventures have been adapted to date by the critically acclaimed graphic artist Jacques Tardi.

[19] This body of work has included a previously unpublished account of a young French soldier's retreat during the defeat of France in May–June 1940, a fragment of a larger project devoted to the war years that was never completed. See Jean Meckert, *La Marche au canon* (Paris: Éditions Joelle Losfeld, 2005).

Select bibliography

Amila, John, *Y a pas de bon dieu!* (Paris: Gallimard, 1950).

Dailly, Yvan, *J'ai bien l'honneur* (Paris: Gallimard, 1951).

Héléna, André, *Les Salauds ont la vie dure!* (Paris: World Press, 1949).

——, *Le Festival des macchabées* (Paris: Armand Fleury, 1951).

——, *Le Condamné à mort* (Paris: Roger Dermée, 1959)

——, *Les Clients du Central Hôtel* (Paris: S.E.P.F.E., 1959).

Malet, Léo, *120, rue de la gare* (Paris: S.E.P.E., 1943). *120, rue de la gare*, trans. Peter Hudson (London: Pan Books Ltd, 1991).

——, *Brouillard au pont Tolbiac* (Paris: Robert Laffront, 1956). *Fog on the Tolbiac Bridge*, trans. Barbara Bray (London: Pan Macmillan Publishers Ltd, 1993).

Meckert, Jean, *Nous avons les mains rouges* (Paris: Gallimard, 1947).

——, *Nous sommes tous des assassins* (Paris: Gallimard, 1952).

Simonin, Albert, *Touchez pas au grisbi!* (Paris: Gallimard, 1953).

Stewart, Terry, *La Mort et l'ange* (Paris: Gallimard, 1948).

——, *La Belle Vie* (Paris: Gallimard, 1950).

Further secondary reading

Emanuel, Michelle, *From Surrealism to Less-Exquisite Cadavers: Léo Malet and the Evolution of the French Roman Noir* (Amsterdam/New York: Rodopi, 2006).

Forbes, Jill and Michael Kelly (eds), *French Cultural Studies: An Introduction* (Oxford: Oxford University Press, 1995).

Gorrara, Claire, *The Roman Noir in Post-War French Culture: Dark Fictions* (Oxford: Oxford University Press, 2003).

Gorrara, Claire, 'Cultural intersections: the American hard-boiled detective novel and early French *roman noir*', *Modern Language Review*, 98/3 (2003), 590–601.

Hewitt, Nicholas (ed.), *The Culture of Reconstruction: European Literature, Thought and Film 1945–1950* (London: Macmillan, 1989).

Kedward, H. R., *La Vie en bleu: France and the French since 1900* (London: Penguin, 2006).

Kelly, Michael, *The Cultural and Intellectual Rebuilding of France after the Second World War* (London: Macmillan/Palgrave, 2004).

Les Temps modernes, 'Pas d'orchidées pour les T. M.', 595 (August–October, 1997).

Mullen, Anne and Emer O'Beirne (eds), *Crime Scenes: Detective Narratives in European Culture since 1945* (Amsterdam: Rodopi, 2000).

4

May 1968, Radical Politics and the Néo-Polar

SUSANNA LEE

The 1960s and 1970s saw a radical evolution in French crime fiction. In the era of May 1968, the *roman noir*, as described in the previous chapter, made way for a more aggressive and politically motivated sub-genre: the *néo-polar*. The term *néo-polar* was coined by one of its early and principal practitioners, Jean-Patrick Manchette, to refer ironically to the 'ersatz' of crime fiction writing and to designate the rapid-fire, politically engaged crime writing that exploded in France in the wake of May 1968 and dominated the French crime fiction scene during the 1970s.[1] In contrast with the fairly staid and structured *roman d'enigme*, and even with the *roman noir*, this emergent crime writing was a markedly more entropic enterprise. Whereas the hard-boiled crime novel saw social justice preserved, if only in the figure of the principal detective, the *néo-polar* took no comfort in either social structures or exemplary individuals. As a movement or trend, it was informed by Manchette's vision of modern crime fiction as writing that 'speaks of the world out of balance, labile, likely to fall down and vanish. Modern crime fiction is the literature of crisis.'[2] The *néo-polar* was born in the late 1960s and early 1970s as a response to – or reflection of – the social unrest of the period. Its principal thematic features are violence, anti-idealism and a focus on marginal individuals. The principal stylistic features of the genre are a graphic vernacular, a rapid narrative pace and a coolly detached tone, even in the face of intense violence.

Manchette is the best known of *néo-polar* authors. His novels include *L'Affaire N'Gustro* (1971), *Laissez bronzer les cadavres*, with Jean-Pierre Bastid (1971), *L'Homme au boulot rouge*, with Barth Jules Sussman (1972), *Nada* (1972), *Ô dingos, ô châteaux* (1972), *Morgue pleine* (1973), *Le Petit Bleu de la côte ouest* (*Three to Kill*, 1976), *Que d'os* (1976), *Fatale* (1977), *La Position du tireur couché* (*The Prone Gunman*, 1981) and *La Princesse du sang* (1996). Some other *néo-polar* authors are Pierre

Siniac, whose novels include *La Nuit des auverpins* (1969), *L'Increvable* (1970), *Deux pourris dans l'île* (1971); Francis Ryck, who wrote *Drôle de pistolet* (1969), *Paris va mourir* (1969), *Testament d'Amérique* (1974); and A.D.G., author of *La Divine Surprise* (1971), *Les Panadeux* (1971), *Cradoque's band* (1972), *La Marche truque* (1972) and *La Nuit des grands chiens malades* (1972).[3] While the *néo-polar* had, by the 1980s, ceased to constitute a distinct crime fiction trend, various writers who continue to publish today are associated with the *néo-polar* family due to the theme and style of their early work. These include, notably, Thierry Jonquet, *Du passé faisons table rase* (1982), *Cours moins vite, camarade, le vieux monde est devant toi!* (1984), *URSS go home!* (1985), all written under the pseudonym of Ramon Mercader; Frédéric Farjardie, *Tueur de flics* (1979), *La Nuit des chats bottés* (1977) and *Gentil Faty!* (1979); and Jean-François Vilar, *C'est toujours les autres qui meurent* (1982) and *Bastille Tango* (1986). The list of *néo-polar* authors given above is not at all exhaustive nor is the list of their individual works.

This chapter presents the *néo-polar* in its historical and social frames. It describes the *néo-polar* as participating in an important cultural conversation, most notably in a vigorous critique of social and political structures. The 'crisis' to which Manchette alluded contains various elements, and I will concentrate on three of these: three important cultural influences that came to bear on the *néo-polar*. The first of these are the student and worker revolutions of May 1968, with their attendant criticisms of authority. The second is a growing consciousness of – and disdain for – rampant commercialism. And the third, less a direct influence than a vital contemporaneous phenomenon, was the rise of the medium of television. In examining these phenomena, I will discuss a representative sample of May 1968-inspired *néo-polars*: Manchette's *Laissez bronzer les cadavres*, *Nada*, *La Position du tireur couché*, *Le Petit Bleu de la côte ouest*, *Ô dingos, ô châteaux* and *Que d'os*, and Francis Ryck's *Testament d'Amérique*.

May 1968

France in the contemporary Anglo-American cultural imagination is often the home of champagne and *haute couture*. But it is also the home of socialist leanings and strong leftist voices, and the greatest recent repository or symbol of these is the May 1968 revolts. People who know almost nothing of France's post-war history have at least heard of May 1968, when academic and political authorities succumbed to a powerful tide of student and worker revolt. The events of May 1968 started with student protests in Nanterre, and then moved to a series of student strikes at universities and even high schools in Paris. After a march on the Sorbonne sparked clashes with police and university administrators, labour unions joined the conflict. A one-day union strike (coinciding with the occupation of the Sorbonne) was followed by sit-in strikes at various manufacturing plants across France (Sud-Aviation in Nantes, Renault in Normandy and elsewhere). By the end of May, six million workers were on strike. The effect of these protests on the socio-political organization of France was profound, if fleeting: President Charles de Gaulle took temporary refuge in Baden-Baden, dissolved the National Assembly and called for new parliamentary elections to take place in June. By the second week in June, however, the unrest had largely dissipated. Street demonstrations were cancelled, and workers returned to their jobs.[4]

The most resounding principle or motivator of the May 1968 revolts was resistance to administrative authority of all stripes: academic, intel-lectual, political and judicial. And with this resistance came a marked preference for action over words and for abolishing rules over improving rules. Consider the graffiti found on the outside of university buildings during the protests: 'On ne revendiquera rien, on ne demandera rien. On prendra, on occupera' (We will claim nothing, we will ask for nothing. We will take, we will occupy). 'Lisez moins, vivez plus' (Read less, live more). 'La société est une plante carnivore' (Society is a carnivorous plant). 'On ne coopère pas avec une société en décomposition' (You don't cooperate with a decomposing society).

The first two slogans point to the comparative worthlessness of words, particularly written words, and underscore the value of action. And all four speak to a radical denial not just of authority, but of *society*, that mere embodiment of public coherence. And yet, of course, these statements are composed of written words: one must read, in order to be told to read less. The sense of action interrupted momentarily in order to be put down in words, and of disorder interrupted momentarily in order to be rendered in narrative form, is intrinsic to the *néo-polar*. Not surprisingly, one of the most notable qualities of the *néo-polar* is a distrust of authorities, be those judicial or intellectual. Another significant element is the absence of an overweening sense of justice in any form. The traditional *roman policier* à la Sherlock Holmes painted an orderly world in which the rule of law seemed both organic and desirable. The body on the carpet was an aberra-tion to be solved, the murderer an anomalous character to be rooted out. With the development of the hard-boiled and the *roman noir* of the 1930s and 1940s, society had become less wholesome, the status quo less clean, the notion of institutional justice less stable. Nonetheless, in the hard-boiled, the idea of justice and principle survived in the figure of the detective. If only by remaining principled and dedicated in his work, the detective compensated for the culture that surrounded him. With the *néo-polar*, though, that beacon of social justice is largely extinguished in a blast of destructive energy – an energy born of social and political discontent. As Margaret Atack writes:

> May 68 forged a collective 'nous' uniting all those excluded and marginalized by bourgeois society and the capitalist state, students, criminals, the young, the Third World, all actual or potential victims. This is also the favourite terrain of *le néo-polar*, a fusion of various kinds of exclusion, as well as a revalorization of the deviant and criminal, promoted to icons of suffering.[5]

And François Cote writes of the genre:

> It is at the start of the 1970s that young novelists take up the torch of political engagement, combining their hard-boiled heritage with other literary genres to forge a style. Jean-Patrick Manchette … fills his narratives with the marginal figures of post-68: leftists, anarchists and neo-fascists, thugs, and *losers*.[6]

The rage of murder, along with the extreme exit from social and humanist norms that murder constitutes, is a prerequisite for the *roman policier* – no crime, no detection – but it is not that genre's actual focal point. Even in the hard-boiled and *roman noir*, murder, an inevitable part of social reality, does not have the relentless presence and pervasiveness that it does in the *néo-polar*. But murderous rage, combined with the indifference of those who have no more use for social structures, is a fundamental characteristic of the *néo-polar*. This sort of crime fiction, in other words, sees the breaking down of beacons of all kinds – of voices, justice, authority and faith in principle. It is not a good-guy genre, for society has become too jaundiced and disordered to allow for a hard-boiled-style good guy. If a good guy presented himself, he would most likely turn out to be a toady of the establishment – a policeman or other functionary; such a good guy would eventually be killed off, as is the case in Manchette's *Laissez bronzer les cadavres* and *Nada*.

Like the May 1968 graffiti cited above, the *néo-polar* is brimming with action but is strikingly slim on moral and intellectual authority. The genre is also short on the sort of neatly wrapped plots that characterized the mystery novel. In *Ô dingos, ô châteaux*, for instance, a woman is released (prematurely, it seems) from a psychiatric hospital and hired by the man who signed her out to care for his young nephew. Shortly following this inauspicious beginning, the woman and the boy are kidnapped. They escape and an exhausting pursuit ensues. At the end, the woman goes back to the hospital before 'getting lost in the vast world'.[7] She never sees the boy again. *Laissez bronzer les cadavres* has a murder spree connected to a robbery; most of the characters, gathered at the remote home of an artist, are too stoned or disoriented to show much shock at the killing. One discombobulated woman tries to steal a car that happens to contain a large amount of gold; numerous people are killed, including two quite decent policemen. Francis Ryck's *Testament d'Amérique* has the main character, Marc, murder the husband of his one-time girlfriend, Julia. The murder seems motivated by jealousy, but Julia is hardly mentioned again; Marc promptly goes to Paris and meets a second woman, Léa. The book then focuses on the relationship between Marc and Léa, who are pursued by the mafia and caught up in the drug addiction of Léa's stepdaughter. Their persecution by the mafia, we learn, has been ordered by Léa's now-deceased ex-husband in America: he had ordered it in his will, the *testament* of the title.

The *néo-polar* is a literature of killing sprees, of absence of narrative closure (at times, Manchette's books seem to end simply because there is almost no one left standing), and, as often as not, a corpus of characters who could not care less about social cohesion. But, to return to the notion of the *néo-polar* as a literature of crisis, let us consider the precise elements of the crisis. On the one hand, we see the crisis of trust in authority and social structures writ large, as embodied in the revolution of May 1968. And in fact, several *néo-polars* were constructed around actual events of the period: Manchette's *L'Affaire N'Gustro*, for instance, is about the disappearance of the Moroccan opposition leader Ben Barka. The narrator of *Nada* (the story of the kidnapping and assassination of an American ambassador by a group of *gauchistes* (left-wing activists) who demand that their manifesto be read in the media) points to the May 1968 graffiti on the walls: 'Tremble you rich your Paris is surrounded we'll burn it'.[8] Indeed, the police in that novel are able to identify the kidnappers from photographs of the May protests. With these historical references, the *néo-polar* stands as a uniquely French form of political writing. As one writer, Jean-Bernard Pouy, puts it: 'Manchette brought in something very important, he brought a specificity to the French novel. For once there were French *noir* novels that were not copies at large of the Anglo-Saxon, American models, but in which there was a true French voice.'[9]

75

In addition to the particularly French phenomenon of May 1968 and its attendant anarchist-Marxist sentiments, the *néo-polar* also taps into a broader (and more broadly European) existential crisis. As much of the 1968 graffiti reveals, the goal of the 1968 revolts was not merely to replace one authority with a better one, but to dismantle the definition of authority – to dismantle the system that made authority what it was. In this sense, the leftist dissatisfactions of 1968 met a larger discontentment – one that Jean-François Lyotard described as the 'postmodern condition'. In his book of that title, Lyotard describes postmodernism as 'incredulity toward metanarratives' – an incredulity that is inextricably intertwined with the collapsing of master narratives after the Second World War.[10] Among the first narratives to be collapsed, not surprisingly, was the story of authority as necessary and unproblematic: a reaction to unspeakable government atrocities. By 1968, it seems, the malaise and mistrust of authorities that was born with the Second World War had spread and become an organic part of life and of narrative. The postmodern condition, channelled in and through 1960s social consciousness, gets felt in the *néo-polar* as a furious but bored existentialism, and narrated as a crime spree that resolutely refuses the comfort and closure of a final righting of things. In keeping with this refusal, the atmosphere of the genre is one less of revolutionary fervour than of nihilism. The dismantling of narratives means that the very idea of teleology – a narrative's orientation toward an end or closure – is denied. In this way, the postmodern condition translates into narrative form.

In this context, salient elements of the *néo-polar* are precisely its directionlessness, its anti-teleology and the hyperactive destructiveness of characters hurtling into a blank future. This directionlessness, shot through with a near-nihilistic distrust of structures, permeates the content and the style of the *néo-polar*. Consider the conclusions to some of the most notable *néo-polars*. At the end of *Laissez bronzer les cadavres*, reinforcements come too late, since almost everyone is dead – and the last word belongs to the village idiot. In *Nada,* from the name of the group to the effect of the assassins, to the zero-sum game of the multiple murders, the effect of this narrative is indeed to return to zero. And, yet, this nothing produces more narratives: the last scene of the book has a Nada member phoning a foreign press agency and offering the story of the group, even as police cars swarm up to his building. *Ô dingos, ô châteaux* finishes when a young nephew calmly leaves the incinerated body of his uncle (the man who had tried to murder him) and goes outside to play Indians. *Testament d'Amérique* ends with (among many other things) the heroine on a plane, bound for a mission of murderous revenge. In *La Position du tireur couché*, the prolific hired gun, Martin Terrier, ends up unable to speak, communicating through notes.[11]

The *néo-polar*'s violent energy and anti-idealism are also manifest in the genre's style and organization. As Kristin Ross writes: 'The very *velocity* of [contemporary French crime fiction], the feverish acceleration in pace of hermeneutic frenzy that plummets the reader head forward to the final moments demands a solid, reliable closure, a reaffirmation of some comforting order and stability in the world.'[12] A review of Manchette's fiction states in a similar vein: 'To call Manchette's style plain would be an understatement ... he writes a cool and lean prose; each sentence exists only to advance from disaster to disaster, or to relay some painful moment from the past.'[13] We find this advancement from disaster to disaster in *Laissez bronzer les cadavres,* which is divided into chapters marked by time of day. Starting at 10.15 in the morning, it recounts a relentless killing spree that ends at 6.30 the following morning. The advancement is headlong indeed; one chapter is entitled 1.20, for instance, and the next, half a page later, 1.21. Nicholas Paige notices this spirit of hurriedness in Manchette's writing and finds in it too an anti-fluid nature; he indicates the author's frequent use of parentheses and proposes that the device is used 'less for the information it transmits than for the hiccups it imposes'.[14] Manchette's writing is as aggressive and relentless as the murders it describes, and his reader can *live* the exhausting movement of the characters through their wasteland. In both style and content, the *néo-polar* enacts a precipitous hurtling into the future – not for the destination, but for the pleasure or energy of the hurtling.

Consumerism

We have mentioned a post-war, postmodern uneasiness that manifests itself in the nihilistic atmosphere of the *néo-polar*. We have considered the critique of authority embodied in 1968, present in the *néo-polar*'s pervasive sense of alienation. But nihilism and alienation have yet another source, and this is consumerism. Here, it seems germane to mention one of the salient philosophical influences on Manchette and other crime authors: the situationists of the 1960s, or members of the Situationist International. A mix of existentialism, Marxism, anarchy and avant-garde art, this movement found its principal theorist in Guy Debord whose 1968 book, *La Société du spectacle*, articulated the alienating quality, the inauthentic nature, of contemporary life. Using as a point of departure the

77

idea of spectacle, Debord describes the persistent obstacles that stand between modern human beings and reality: 'Everything that had been directly lived has moved off into a representation.'[15] This is the opening line, but it becomes clear that the spectacle is not a hermeneutic theory but an actual political and social tool. 'The spectacle is not an ensemble of images, but a social connection among people, mediated by images.'[16] And, in a statement reminiscent of Manchette's narrative anti-teleologies: 'Society built on modern industry ... is fundamentally *spectacliste*. In spectacle, itself an image of the reigning economy, the goal is nothing, and development is everything.'[17] The book includes more than two hundred blurbs on the notion of the spectacle, as everything from a force of alienation to a tool of forced social unification, to the essence and instrument of political manipulation.

Essential to the situationist *propos* is the notion of resistance to an agenda, resistance to description or encapsulation from without. The situationist manifesto, however, does not just restate postmodern distrust of metanarratives, but also addresses a more concrete and present disingenuousness: the force of consumerist culture. Consumerism, for Debord, has infused modern life, public and private, with triteness and a sense of manipulation. In this sense, situationism joins May 1968 in the desire to forge an original path, to refuse the road already taken by an earlier generation. And this is not only because the earlier generation was oppressive, but also because it was oppressed – because it had absorbed formulaic ideas about work, authority and education that the 1968 generation longed to topple. The *néo-polar* plugs into this longing, and much of the alienation embodied in the genre has to do with what Debord calls a *spectacliste* society: a distancing from what is authentic. The *néo-polar*, like the situationists, is engaged in a vigorous critique of consumerist culture. Thus, the genre frequently shows characters in aggressive encounters with the emporiums and symbols of consumerism; the discount store, for instance, that most unremarkable of spaces and places, is a recurring site of bedlam in the *néo-polar* genre. In *Ô dingos, ô châteaux*, the astonishingly chaotic central chase scene (an excerpt from which is included at the end of this chapter) happens in a Prisunic, a sort of French version of Woolworths. Here, the society of the spectacle meets postmodern alienation meets hippie social consciousness: Joan Baez is playing on the store's sound system as the main female protagonist and her young charge barrel through the store, pursued by the killers, flinging items onto the floor as obstacles. Eventually, the entire store catches fire.[18]

Guy Debord's critique of the 'society of the spectacle' is fully connected to the notion of disingenuous representation – to the idea of images that simulate and ultimately substitute for reality. He essentially describes a world in which everything, as a result of being rendered again and again as spectacle, is made alien, enveloped in a shroud of falsehood and capitalist manipulation. As Serge Quadruppani describes:

> At the end of his life [situationism's] most well known representative, Guy Debord, was transformed by the media and the literary hype, and one might also say by his own collaboration, into a kind of haughty dandy figure, contemptuous of his time and devoid of any hope of social transformation. But to reduce Debord to that is to forget that the first paragraphs of the book, *La Société du spectacle*, by which he marked his era, are a tracing, a "détournement" (a "re-routing"), as it was called then, of the first pages of *Das Kapital.*[19]

While a *spectacliste* society participates in consumerist falsification, the *néo-polar* aims to combat it. A *spectacliste* society is anti-art, a deadening force; the *néo-polar* shocks it back to life.

Television

It is worth noting that the rise of television in France paralleled the rise of the *néo-polar*, creating points of intersection between form and media. The classic *roman noir*, as has often been pointed out in criticism, has much in common with the art of cinema. And indeed, many *romans noirs* became movies. So too did many *néo-polars*.[20] Guy Debord's *La Société du spectacle* also became a movie, consisting of a monotone recitation of certain passages against a background of stock images, including images of May 1968. The late 1960s and early 1970s *néo-polar* that we are discussing here is awash with certain cinematographic qualities. Television shares with cinema a focus on the visual, on action, dialogue, momentum, stimulation, narrative form. But it also differs from cinema on several important points that are relevant to the *néo-polar*. First, its narratives play out in a short form, in half-hour or one-hour segments. Secondly, television is more likely than cinema to represent the banalities of domestic living. Thirdly, it represents an incessant and serial form of representation. Fourthly, and significantly, French television narratives have, since the era of the *néo-polar*, been interspersed with commercials.

Television is the medium par excellence both of repetitive images and of rapid scene changes. If one were close enough to the television to change the channel (an operation now made effortless with remote control), one could see a bland household scene, a shoot-'em-up and a talking horse all in the space of a few seconds. This same cacophonous variety appears in the *néo-polar*; but, whereas television at least makes these scenes consecutive, the *néo-polar* piles them on top of one another and encourages the one to contaminate the other.

Television, furthermore, makes a spectacle of the banal in much the same way as the *néo-polar*. The *néo-polar* is not particularly rich in cinematic *ambiance*, at least not the way that the *roman noir* and hard-boiled fiction of the 1930s and 1940s were. In those earlier forms, subversive behaviour snuck around the back alleys under the cover of darkness: this was the seamy underbelly of the world, the dangerous side that the detective was there to negotiate. By the time the *néo-polar* comes onto the scene, though, there is no more underbelly – or perhaps it is more precise to say that there is nothing that is *not* underbelly. Much of the action of the *néo-polar* takes place during the daytime, in run-of-the-mill living rooms, busy streets and stores. The principal character of Francis Ryck's *Testament d'Amérique* spends a lot of time sitting around the living room of an average apartment in the fifteenth *arrondissement* of Paris. In *Le Petit Bleu de la côte ouest*, two assassins try to murder the main character while he is in the water on a beach vacation, splashing around among other vacationing families. Neither the rule of law nor a social moral code nor the sanctity of the domestic sphere, nor even the ethics or passion of one individual is strong enough to keep the contamination of violence at bay, either at the level of plot or at the level of atmosphere. Violence can penetrate the most mundane places because there is no place and no force strong enough to contain it or resist it. The 'crisis' of which the *néo-polar* is the literary expression can be read as a crisis of violence, but first and foremost it is a crisis of disenchantment and of boredom that results, in a sense, from an overload of images – from the very overload of *spectaclisme* embodied in television.

This crisis of boredom leads us to another element of television pertinent to the *néo-polar*: the medium's incessant nature, both in its serial format (the gunslinger of this afternoon's episode will be on again tomorrow or next week at the same time) and in its continuous programming. When a movie is over, the audience leaves the cinema and goes elsewhere. But television, although its narratives come in a short form, can go on hour after hour after hour. *Néo-polar* narratives have the same unremitting quality: the sense that if the story ends, it is not because closure has been reached, or a problem resolved, but simply because it was time to end that particular episode. *Que d'os* terminates with the narrator claiming fatigue and *La*

Position du tireur couché ends with the hero asleep; but this is not the sleep of closure: rather, the sleep of a momentary respite, for, as we are told, our hero sleeps in the prone firing position. The ticking chapter clock in *Laissez bronzer les cadavres*, similarly, does not give a sense of time ordered and divided, but of time racing forward into nothing. When the narrator of *Nada* tells us that a killing spree had taken less than half an hour, it does not seem that something finite has been accomplished, but rather that we are rushing on to the next action, the next spree.

To return to the idea of the spectacle and of a relentless commodification of human existence, one of the most important differences between post-1968 television and cinema is, of course, the presence of commercials in television. Television was and is fuelled by advertising, and the commodity it represents (entertainment, escape from boredom, access to information) is inextricably intertwined with the commodities that it channels (products, products and more products). The *néo-polar* serves to explode this connection, sometimes literally – which suggests that the *néo-polar* also represents a crisis of irritation at a consumerist culture. In the midst of the chase scene through the Prisunic in *Ô dingos, ô châteaux*, the author pauses to inform us that a set of unbreakable plates does in fact remain intact when thrown on the ground. Violence, speed, the banality of commercialism, the meaningless durability of mass-produced homeware, the lilting but processed sounds of 1960s folk music and death – all meet in the space of a few pages. Product placement in this scene of bedlam underscores the *néo-polar*'s criticism of commercialism, and when the entire store goes up in flames, one assumes, the plates go with it.

In conclusion, the authors and novels discussed in this chapter are examples of the *néo-polar*, the French crime fiction genre that was born around and from the revolts of May 1968. These authors took that era's disaffection and resistance to authority and rendered them in narrative form. For some *néo-polar* authors, the unrest of 1968 became part of their novels' thematic content. For many others, it manifested itself in an atmosphere of anger and boredom, in a rapid narration, in an absence of closures and solutions and, most notably, in explosions of violence. These are the characteristic features of the *néo-polar* – the features that mark its departure from the less bleak and visceral crime fiction of earlier decades. Despite – or more likely because of – its representation of a 'decomposing society', the *néo-polar* has begun to receive considerable critical attention and to be read in the academy. This literature, it has been recognized, provides a valuable window onto the social and cultural phenomena of the late twentieth century – a window, that is, on the crises of its time.

* * *

Extract from Jean-Patrick Manchette's *Ô dingos, ô châteaux*

Thompson and Coco, two hit men/kidnappers, are pursuing Julie, a psychi-
atric patient turned babysitter, and her young charge, Peter, through a
Prisunic. Julie has ordered a saleswoman to call the police, but it is too late;
Thompson and Coco are on her heels. This chapter contains the trademark
néo-polar *qualities of rapid-fire narration, casual references to gruesome*
violence, loud explosions and an ironic view of commercialism and
consumerism.

Thompson decided he could wait no longer. With bewildering rapidity, the
store was turning into a mental asylum. More and more people began
running. A trail of debris lay in the aisles where Julie had passed. Women
were shrieking. Several sales ladies had begun ringing their little bells,
normally meant to summon a manager to give change or verify the identity
of a customer paying by cheque. Above the pandemonium floated the serene
but booming voice of mother Baez, diffused over the loud-speaker as background music. It was bedlam.

Thompson had stretched out his arm, and his stomach hurt so badly he
thought he would tear in half, and Julie's silhouette started into the gun's
sight. The girl fell on the ground. Thompson increased his fire through the
frenzied crowd. The second projectile (a 9 mm Parabellum) blew to bits the
head of a frantic customer. The man had been running, he threw his arms in
front of him like a diver and belly-flopped onto the store's floor. Thompson
shivered. His stomach was like a giant ball of fire. His nostrils dilated at the
smell of the gunpowder. He hadn't been paying attention to the explosions.
But all around him, the crowd had gone absolutely nuts. People went by
running and shouting, between Julie on the ground and the automatic
tracking her. Thompson could see neither Julie nor Peter. He dashed into an
aisle, knocking over an old lady who began weeping in terror. He ran into the
children's department, his mouth full of bile. He heard a deafening explosion
and supposed that Coco had decided to open fire. Bits of plastic flew over the
displays. An enormous tumult rose from the store. This is exciting, I'm
excited, mused Thompson, spitting bile on the floor. More and more people
were on the ground, huddled against the base of the shelves. Mothers lay on
their children to protect them. Everyone was howling. Thompson was
laughing like a hyena.

Jean-Patrick Manchette, *Romans noirs* (Paris: Gallimard, 2005), trans.
Susanna Lee, pp. 300–1.

Notes

1. 'Dès 1979, la presse parle de *néopolar*, terme inventé ironiquement par Manchette pour désigner les ersatzs de la production policière. Mais c'est avec sérieux que la presse le désigne comme le père fondateur de ce courant qui comporte des auteurs post années 70 traitant des préoccupations sociales ou politiques' (*www.manchette.rayonpolar.com*). As Manchette puts it in a 1981 article, 'J'ai formé alors le mot "néopolar", sur le modèle de mots de "néopain", "néovin" ou même "néoprésident", par quoi la critique radicale désigne les ersatz qui, sous un nom illustre, ont partout remplacé la même chose' (I fashioned the word 'néopolar' after words like 'neo-bread', 'neo-wine', or even 'neo-president', which radical critics use to designate the substitutes that, though under a lofty name, just replace the same thing), *Chroniques* (Paris: Éditions Payot et Rivages, 1996), p. 200.

2. '… [C]ause d'un monde déséquilbré, donc labile, appelé donc à tomber et à passer. Le polar est la littérature de la crise', Manchette, *Chroniques*, p. 53.

3. This chapter concentrates on social critiques in the Marxist vein, or at least in the leftist vein. And most of the writers associated with the *néo-polar* genre are on the leftist side of the political spectrum, but not all. A.D.G., *nom de plume* of Alain Fournier, is not only not left wing, he belongs to the extreme right and served as the editor in chief at *Rivarol*, an extreme right-wing newspaper. A.D.G.'s *La Nuit des grands chiens malades* has the narrator – a villager in what seems to be a redneck French backwater – comment on a visiting band of hippies: 'They set fire to cars in May 1968 and that year was definitely the year of the devil, because nothing worked like it was supposed to, livestock died, lots of milk turned, the little wine we had wasn't good, and the crops were scrawny' (author's translation, p. 12). In the last pages of the narrative, the narrator attempts suicide, at which point another character picks up the story and reveals that the first narrator had been speaking to us from an asylum.

4. See Adrien Dansette, *Mai 1968* (Paris: Plon, 1971), for an overview of the events of May 1968.

5. Margaret Atack, *May 68 in French Fiction and Film: Rethinking Society, Rethinking Representation* (Oxford: Oxford University Press, 1999), p. 135.

6. 'C'est au début des années 70 que de jeunes romanciers reprennent le flambeau de la contestation, en combinant l'héritage hard-boiled et d'autres genres littéraires sur le plan du style. Jean-Patrick Manchette, l'un des pionniers du genre, fait figurer dans ses récits les nouveaux marginaux de l'après-68: gauchistes, anarchistes et néo-fascistes; loubards et *losers*.' François Cote, 'Le néo-polar français et les policiers', *Esprit*, 135 (February 1988), 135 (author's italics).

7. 'Avant de se perdre dans le vaste monde', *Romans noirs*, p. 335. All subsequent Manchette quotations are from the Gallimard collection of his work, *Romans noirs* (2005).

8. 'Tremblez riches votre Paris est encerclé on le brûlera', p. 414. Manchette

writes in his journal: 'Relu *L'Affaire N'Gustro*. Très violent et ordurier. Imparfait, surtout en ce qui concerne la fin. Heureusement, de nos jours, l'imperfection plaît. Penser à mettre un bref avertissement, à peu près ainsi conçu; *L'Affaire N'Gustro* inclut des faits ressemblant fort à certains de ceux qui aboutirent à la disparition de Ben Barka.' (Reread *L'Affaire N'Gustro*. Very violent and filthy. Imperfect, especially the ending. Fortunately, these days, imperfection is in. Think about inserting a brief notice, along these lines: *L'Affaire N'Gustro* includes facts that resemble those that led to the disappearance of Ben Barka), *Romans noirs*, p. 121.

9   Interview with Jean-Bernard Pouy by Elfriede Müller, 29 January 2004, trans. Steve Novak, *www.europolar.eu.*

10   Jean-François Lyotard, *The Postmodern Condition* (Minneapolis: University of Minnesota Press, 1984), p. xxiv.

11   Nicholas Paige reads the silence of this main character as reflective of the silence of the author, who published nothing between *La Position du tireur couché* and his death fourteen years later. See Nicholas Paige, 'Manchette, ou le mutisme', *Poétique*, 120 (1999), 477–94 (477).

12   Kristin Ross, 'Watching the detectives', in F. Barker, P. Hulme and M. Iversen (eds), *Postmodernism and the Re-Reading of Modernity* (Manchester: Manchester University Press, 1992), pp. 46–65.

13   Hillary Frey, 'The pleasures of crime', *The Nation* (15 March 2004), 30.

14   '[M]oins pour l'information qu'il véhicule que pour le rythme de hoquet qu'il impose', Paige, 'Manchette, ou le mutisme', 485.

15   'Tout ce qui était directement vécu s'est éloigné dans une représentation', Guy Debord, *La Société du spectacle* (Paris: Éditions Champ Libre, 1971), p. 9.

16   'Le spectacle n'est pas un ensemble d'images, mais un rapport social entre des personnes, médiatisé par des images', Debord, *La Société du spectacle*, p. 10.

17   'La société qui repose sur l'industrie moderne ... est fondamentalement *spectacliste*. Dans le spectacle, image de l'économie régnante, le but n'est rien, le développement est tout', Debord, *La Société du spectacle*, p. 13 (author's italics).

18   Daniel Pennac's *Au bonheur des ogres* (*The Scapegoat*, 1985), based very loosely on Emile Zola's novelistic tribute to the department store, has a similarly frenzied series of explosions taking place in a Monoprix.

19   Serge Quadruppani, 'Jean-Patrick Manchette, radical writing', trans. Steve Novak. *www.europolar.eu.* (translation modified by the author of this chapter).

20   Most of Manchette's novels were made into movies, among them *Ô dingos, ô châteaux* as *Folle à tuer* (1975), *La Position du tireur couché* as *Le Choc* (1982), and *Que d'os* as *Pour la peau d'un flic* (1982). So too were several novels by Francis Ryck, Pierre Siniac, Frédéric Farjardie, Jean-François Vilar and other *néo-polar* authors.

Select bibliography

A.D.G., *La Nuit des grands chiens malades* (Paris: Gallimard, 1972).

Manchette, Jean-Patrick, *L'Affaire N'Gustro* (Paris: Gallimard, 1971).

——, *Nada* (Paris: Gallimard, 1972).

——, *Ô dingos, ô châteaux* (Paris: Gallimard, 1972).

——, *Morgue pleine* (Paris: Gallimard, 1973).

——, *Que d'os* (Paris: Gallimard, 1976).

——, *Fatale* (Paris: Gallimard, 1977).

——, *Le Petit Bleu de la côte ouest* (Paris: Gallimard, 1976). *Three to Kill*, trans. Donald Nicolson-Smith (San Francisco: City Lights, 2002).

——, *La Position du tireur couché* (Paris: Gallimard, 1981). *The Prone Gunman*, trans. James Brook (London: Serpent's Tail, 2006).

——, *Romans noirs* (Paris: Gallimard, 2005).

Manchette, Jean-Patrick and Jean-Pierre Bastid, *Laissez bronzer les cadavres* (Paris: Gallimard, 1971).

Manchette, Jean-Patrick and Barth Jules Sussman, *L'Homme au boulot rouge* (Paris Gallimard, 1972).

Ryck, Francis, *Testament d'Amérique* (Paris: Gallimard, 1974).

Further secondary reading

Internationale Situationniste: édition augmentée (Paris: Librairie Arthème Fayard, 1997).

Deloux, Jean-Pierre, 'Polar à la française: treize ans de bonheur!', *Magazine Littéraire*, 344 (June 1996), 22–5.

Gorrara, Claire, 'Reflections on crime and punishment: memories of the Holocaust in recent French crime fiction', *Yale French Studies*, 108 (2005), 131–45.

Lee, Susanna, 'Punk *noir*: anarchy in two idioms', *Yale French Studies*, 108 (2005), 177–88.

Reuter, Yves, *Le Roman policier et ses personnages* (Saint-Denis, France: Presses Universitaires de Vincennes, 1989).

5

Gender and Genre: Women in French Crime Writing

VÉRONIQUE DESNAIN

Reading the numerous articles which came out in the French press in the 1980s and 1990s, it would be easy to conclude that French crime writers had been, until then, exclusively male. Suddenly, *le polar féminin* (women's crime writing) was being discussed at length and female authors were lauded as pioneers. Such a presentation, however, is based on a fallacy and opens the door to a number of issues. This chapter will examine the place of female authors in French crime writing from its inception to the present day. In doing so, it will attempt to dispel a number of misconceptions regarding the presence of women in particular genres, their styles and aims and, perhaps most importantly, the notion that 'women's crime writing' constitutes a genre distinct from all others. In the course of doing this, we will also look at specific texts in order to exemplify the theories put forward and to familiarize the reader with the work of a few of the most prominent female proponents of contemporary French crime writing.

A short history of women's crime writing in France

Unlike the USA, where some of the first crime writers were women, such as Anna Katharina Green with *The Leavenworth Case* (1878) and Mary Roberts Rhinehart with *The Spiral Staircase* (1908), or the UK, where the reputation of Agatha Christie, P. D. James and others often exceeds that of their male counterparts, France appears to have produced few female crime writers until the early 1980s. This impression, however, can easily be disproved. A study by Deborah Hamilton has found over 140 female writers and about 1,750 texts by women published in France between the 1920s and the 1990s.[1] One of the most notable early works was penned by Camille Hedwige who introduced, as early as 1935–6 in *L'Appel de la morte*, a female sleuth. A true perception of the impact of women in crime writing up to recent years is also impeded by the fact that few of them are mentioned in historical accounts of the genre and many found it useful (or were forced by publishers such as Fleuve Noir) to use male pseudonyms. Only the most vigilant of readers would be aware that authors such as George Tiffany, Mike Cooper or the prolific Mario Ropp were both French and female. Nonetheless, a quick search of archives shows that women have contributed to the genre fairly regularly from the start. From the 1930s, we find Miriam Dou, Juliette Pary and Suzanne Frémont. Odette Sorensen published her first crime novel, *Drame en Sorbonne*, under the pseudonym Luc Rivière in 1943 and won the most prestigious literary prize for crime fiction in France, the Grand Prix de la Littérature Policière, for *La Parole est au mort* in 1949. Antoinette Soulas appears in the late 1950s (*Mort d'une ombre,* 1958). These few names are given by way of example and can be said to represent only the tip of the iceberg that is women's contribution to French crime writing from the 1930s to the late 1960s.

More recently, authors such as Janine Oriano (the first French woman to be published in the famous Série Noire in 1971), Noëlle Loriot (who won the Grand Prix de la Littérature Policière in 1966), Catherine Arley, Hélène de Monaghan and Madeleine Coudray all first made their mark on French crime writing during the 1960s and 1970s with a wide range of titles while many more published one or two titles before disappearing. Already, a quick survey of some of those authors suggests that their work is as varied as it is abundant and successful: Catherine Arley was published mostly in suspense collections but her thrillers are marked by humour and a wilful subversion of clichés. Monaghan also injects humour into her *romans de détection* (detective novels), often by employing unlikely investigators. While her Corsican police inspector Pline Matucchi (a caricature of the French southern male who is an obsessive fisherman and the frequent unrequited suitor of blonde goddesses) appears in several novels, the detective is just as likely to be rather less of a professional: thus the investigation is led by a charlatan fortune teller in *Vacances éternelles* (1974) or by a pro-death penalty retired female judge in *Le Couperet* (1987). The author also eschews some of the traditional rules of the whodunnit: in *Esprit de suite* (1972), the narrator is none other than the criminal himself, or rather the potential criminal since the narrative follows his increasingly frantic but always unsuccessful attempts to get rid of his wife, before falling victim to his mother-in-law's murderous ploy. It must be noted that the comic elements of Monaghan's novels often serve to make more palatable some fairly barbed comments about society in general and gender relations in particular. Finally, Noëlle Loriot, who also wrote suspense novels under the pseudonym of Laurence Oriol, is probably best known for her novel *Docteur Françoise Gailland*, adapted for the cinema in 1975–6, and for *Le Juge est une femme*, a television series based on her Florence Larrieu series of novels. Larrieu is a young female judge, trying to balance work and private life. In the course of her job, she is brought to explore different milieux (television production, hospitals, publishing) which, despite their variety, have one thing in common: they are peopled by the members of the *haute bourgeoisie* (the French upper classes). Through these novels, Loriot exposes the hypocrisy and greed of the upper echelons of society, their attempts to hold on to the power offered by birth and money but also the pressures suffered by some of the members of this class. To a large extent, the title of her 2004 novel, *Meurtrière bourgeoisie* (lethal bourgeoisie), could be said to sum up the majority of her œuvre.

However, it was in the 1980s and 1990s that a new generation of women writers came to prominence: Fred Vargas, Andrea H. Japp, Maud Tabachnik, Brigitte Aubert, Dominique Manotti, Sylvie Granotier, Chantal Pelletier, Dominique Sylvain, Claude Amoz, Virginie Brac and Pascale Fonteneau, to name but a few. They finally brought crime fiction by women to the attention of a wider audience and, perhaps more significantly, managed to make their mark in genres and collections which were previously seen as the exclusive preserve of male writers.

This reference to collections is important: it is symptomatic of the French market that collections exercise editorial pressure to ensure that their production fits a particular image. Such policies could clearly be detrimental to new writers, since, as pointed out by Michel Amelin, they put the emphasis on a specific house style rather than individual talent and originality.[2] They also have had an impact on whether women were published in particular collections: The famous Série Noire, for example, was perceived as tough, gritty writing in the American *noir* mould (translations of writers such as Chandler, Hammett and Himes constitute a large part of its catalogue) and therefore unsuitable for women writers. Raymond Queneau's assertion that, in the Série Noire, 'violence and brutality have replaced scientific deductions and ... women all have fantastic legs, are perfidious and untrustworthy'[3] suggests that it was clearly focused on a male perspective. Conversely, Le Masque, which publishes Agatha Christie in France and started publishing French women writers in 1930, three years after it was created, was seen as specializing in more 'gentle', non-violent whodunnit narratives and therefore ideally suited to female writers. The problem was twofold: editors in particular collections may have seen novels by women as unsuitable for their series due to their own preconceptions regarding 'women's writing' and female writers would assume that their work would be rejected by particular collections because of their reputation as male bastions and therefore did not approach them, hence reinforcing the notion that women were not suited to writing in particular genres. For the Série Noire, the problem came to a head under the editorship of Patrick Raynal, who, tired of being accused of sexism, actively sought to publish women writers and put out a call for manuscripts to that effect. Among the first to benefit from this proactive policy were Pascale Fonteneau (*Confidences sur l'escalier*, 1992 and *États de lame*, 1993), Alix de Saint André (*L'Ange et le réservoir de liquide à freins*, 1994), Sylvie Granotier (*Sueurs chaudes*, 1997) and Chantal Pelletier (*Eros et Thalasso*, 1998). All of them, with the exception of Saint André, are now established crime writers and are opening new avenues in collections traditionally concerned with macho detectives, dangerous women and graphic violence. It was in the early 1990s that media and critical attention started focusing, not on individual authors, but on the so-called *polar féminin*.

Gender and genre

The terminology itself is problematic: *le polar féminin* defines the gender of the author but could as easily be understood to define a genre for female readers. It also seems to imply that crime fiction written by women can be perceived as a singular, distinct genre, regardless of the variety of approaches, styles and topics represented within it, despite the fact that many of these writers could be more usefully identified as belonging to particular sub-genres, such as *noir* fiction, political thrillers and suspense. In other words, it suggests that crime writing by women is possessed of qualities which can first be recognized as specific to all female writers and, possibly, as absent from the work of male writers. Amelin's article, written in 1984, tells us that Jeanine Merlin's work is the apogee of female crime writing in the 1960s.[4] This gives us no indication of her place within crime literature more generally, or indeed any information about whether her novels are whodunnits, thrillers or *noir* and how she might compare with male writers in those fields. Such examples abound: the specialist website *noir comme polar* is fairly typical in proposing an 'ideal library' in which two of the categories are *Aujourd'hui* (contemporary novels), which does not include any female writers, and *Affaire de femme* (women writers), which does not include any French authors. Dominique Manotti, one of the most prominent writers of recent years, expressed her outrage at this reductive approach in an article in which she states:

> Any number of debates led by men take place on the subject of film and crime writing, the artistic quality, the style, sociology and so on of crime writing. Meanwhile we [female writers] are constantly asked to talk about women and crime writing. It is a way of confining us to the notion of the eternal feminine.[5]

Despite these attempts to label female writers solely according to their gender, an overview of some of them quickly reveals that the field is far from unified, although it must be noted that many of the most prominent among them show a predilection for *noir* fiction. Ironically, it is perhaps the very rigidity of the rules of crime writing (and therefore the potential for perverting them) and its rather old-fashioned, misogynistic approach to gender that attract female authors. As seen in chapter 6 of this volume, strict rules offer great potential for deconstruction and parody. It is therefore no surprise that female authors should have honed in on a genre which has until recently been fraught with macho clichés and androcentric preoccupations. It could easily be argued that French crime writing in general has a long tradition of stereotyping female characters: from Madame Maigret to the femme fatale, they are either comforting side-kicks to the real detectives, dangerously seductive foes or, worse still, anonymous victims. Many female writers admit to being avid crime readers and having been disappointed by the lack of realistic female characters. This stereotyping and the lack of realistic representations of women has prompted some female writers to develop their own complex female protagonists who are far closer to the reality of women's lives. Furthermore, the codification of crime writing provides a useful basis to challenge some of the assumptions regarding the balance of power between genders. With its reliance on accepted notions of right and wrong, its focus on transgression and its drive towards the restoration of order, crime writing inevitably reveals, when read from a gendered perspective, the double standards, failures and prejudices which drive the justice system and society in general.

As Hamilton points out, 'despite an almost total lack of knowledge about each other among the writers themselves, a study of French women writers' texts with female sleuths reveals a continuity of concerns explicitly challenging the underlying assumptions of the male-dominated French detective-fiction tradition'.[6] One of the first to do so was Camille

Hedwige. Her 1936 novel *L'Appel de la morte* is groundbreaking not in its presentation of a female sleuth, since French readers were already familiar with such characters from reading anglophone writers such as Agatha Christie and Dorothy L. Sayers, but in the way both its structure and its themes reveal the gender bias encoded within the genre.

The first section of the narrative presents itself as a fairly straightforward crime story: the body of a drowned woman is found in a lake. The police are called in to investigate, collecting clues and talking to witnesses in typical whodunnit style. The narrative then takes a less conventional direction when the central character, Antoinette Ambre, is prompted to investigate after conflicting clues have rendered the 'scientific' resolution impossible: unable to assert whether the death is a murder or a suicide, the police have closed the case. With this failure of the official detectives, the narrative moves onto a different level, one in which the gender of the investigator takes on its full meaning. Antoinette takes the investigation away from the scene of the crime and into the home of the victim. There her progress is impeded by two factors: first, she is not part of the official apparatus, one in which science and knowledge are perceived as essentially male qualities and, consequently, the clues she unearths are dismissed as insignificant. Secondly, and more importantly, she finds herself confronted with a rural, aristocratic society which closes rank to protect one of its own. This microcosm of society is dependent for its survival on the preservation of male hegemony (land and fortune are passed on from fathers to sons) and the safeguarding of appearances. As Hamilton asserts: 'Hedwige further demonstrates how the gender divide transcends socio-cultural divisions by generalising the category of victim and by exploring its implications, another break from the structure of the classic detective novel that required only minimal characterisation of the victim.'[7] When Antoinette discovers that the husband of the dead woman was violently possessive of his wife and children, this is considered insufficient evidence to see him as a suspect by the *commissaire* (superintendent) in charge but, impelled by both her identification with the victim and her fear that the drowned woman's daughter may eventually suffer a similar fate, she continues her enquiries and reveals the culprit. By the end of the book, Antoinette has solved the murder, adopted the daughter of the victim and, most importantly, turned down a possible relationship with the *commissaire* to pursue her career and life as a single mother, a highly unusual path for a woman of her time and class. With this novel, Hedwige twists the traditional narrative to emphasize the links between the private and public realms, to posit the victim as one of the most important characters and to demonstrate 'that, despite the progressive ideology's promise of equality and universality, Antoinette's marginalisation within the official investigation parallels the limitations placed on women's roles in a more traditional order'.[8] The unusual structure both reveals the assumptions of the conventional crime novel and reflects the radical choices made by the heroine.

Sixty years later, a similar argument could be made about Brigitte Aubert's main character in *La Mort des bois* (*Death from the Woods*, 1996) and *La Mort des neiges* (*Death from the Snows*, 2000): Elise has been rendered quadriplegic, blind and dumb by a terrorist bomb. Despite the obvious obstacle of her disabilities, she finds herself investigating, and solving, a series of murders in each of the books. Aubert's choice of heroine may at first glance appear to be a self-inflicted challenge from a prolific author who has tackled, and often parodied, every genre of the crime narrative, from the whodunnit (*Les Quatre Fils du Dr March*, 1992) to the thriller (*La Rose de fer*, 1993). Yet the position of Elise, dismissed, over-protected and threatened because of her condition, could be seen as an extreme allegory for the position of the female sleuth. Her internal monologue makes it clear that the limitations imposed on her by those guided by their own preconceptions regarding her abilities are unwarranted and she has to fight those, as much as the criminals, in order to bring her investigations to a satisfactory conclusion.

It would be too easy nonetheless to conclude that female writers necessarily challenge stereotypes. Janine Oriano's *B comme Baptiste* (1971) was the first book by a French woman published in the Série Noire. In it, the male narrator finds himself navigating between two stock characters: his overbearing matronly wife, Madeleine, who is nicknamed *la grosse* (fatty) and the dangerous young temptress, Sandrine, designated as *la gosse* (the kid). While the two opposing clichés already offer a limited panorama of femininity, one close to the mother/whore denounced by early feminists such as Simone de Beauvoir, they can also be seen as belonging to a continuum in which women are seen, depending on their age and their relationship to the male narrator, first as desirable, then as a burden. Noreiko points out the similarity between *grosse* and *gosse* and concludes that 'this fortuitous similarity between the two words takes significance in this context: it unites the comfortable but claustrophobic Madeleine with her younger sister, the captivating Sandrine, as the two ends of one process: all women, it implies, are basically the same.'[9]

It is clear that creating a female character within the crime genre is a loaded exercise and some authors have deliberately put the emphasis on

male characters in order to prevent readers projecting their own preconceptions on to female characters. The argument developed by Fred Vargas
is that, while in the public's mind the male character is neutral, any female
character is inevitably going to be categorized according to a handful of
stereotypes.[10] No particular expectations or qualities are ascribed to a
male hero whereas a woman is immediately assimilated to one of thirty
or more possible roles which are virtually impossible for a writer to
counteract: from 'the whinger' to 'the mother', from 'the victim' to 'the
bitch', the female character's actions will be interpreted to fit one of those
stereotypes. Vargas therefore found it almost impossible to create a female
protagonist at the beginning of her career. She later made a deliberate
attempt to do so with Camille in *L'Homme à l'envers* (*Seeking Whom He
May Devour*, 1999) and has recently continued to introduce female characters who are deliberately at odds with traditional notions of femininity
(such as Camille, a plumber/composer, or her mother, a famous oceanog-
rapher) and to give them a more prominent role but her main protagonist
remains the recurrent figure of *commissaire* Adamsberg.

Others have also attempted, with more or less success, to counteract the
stereotype. For the most part French writers do not, unlike their American
counterparts such as Sara Paretsky, create wish-fulfilling, superhuman
female figures, and many are in fact very critical of this approach, which
they see as too formulaic. Rather, they present women who are at once
victims, survivors and avengers. Few of the characters written by women
are professional investigators. When they are, they are either male
(Vargas's Adamsberg and Kehlweiler, Manotti's *commissaire* Daquin) or
rather unrealistic (Dominique Sylvain's Louise Morvan in the series that
started with *Baka!* in 1995, and now totals five volumes, or Evane
Hanska's private detective in *La Raison du plus mort*, 1999). A notable
exception to this is the work of Danielle Thiéry, herself a former *commissaire*, who created a literary alter ego, Edwige Marion, whose career is
strangely similar to that of the author. In almost all cases, however, the
investigators created by contemporary female writers bear little resemblance to their traditional predecessors: Aubert offers us a transvestite and
a blind quadriplegic, Manotti a gay police inspector, Maud Tabachnik a
Jewish policeman with an overbearing mother and a passion for fashion as
well as a lesbian journalist, Andrea H. Japp a love-struck FBI agent and a
paranoid alcoholic mathematical genius, and Virginie Brac a hermaphro-
dite. Of course, this effort to renew characterization could also be said to
be true of contemporary male writers but a closer look reveals that it often
enables female writers to expose particular gender issues as well as giving

them an opportunity to expose certain features of the crime genre. In Brigitte Aubert's *Transfixions* (1998) and *Une âme de trop* (2006) and Virginie Brac's *Tropique du pervers* (2000) the narratives question the very notion of femininity through, respectively, transvestism/transsexuality, split personalities and hermaphrodism. The sexual abuse of women and children are common themes and an important part of the characterization of Gloria Parker-Simmons in Andrea H. Japp's series. The interference of love also disturbs the traditional narrative (in which the investigator should be neutral and entirely focused on resolution). It is the case, for example, in Manotti's *Sombre sentier* (*Rough Trade*, 1995) in which Daquin's involvement with an illegal worker and informant both helps and hinder his enquiries while his homosexuality also means that he is marginalized in his professional milieu.

This notion of marginality is perhaps one of the aspects which do in fact attract women to *noir* writing: the lone wolf of American fiction is not dissimilar to the disenfranchised women who must resort to cunning rather than official channels in their search for justice and who are constantly confronted with obstacles put in their way by a male-centred society that recognizes neither their right to investigate nor the validity of their complaints. Thus the 'amateur' and outsider status of the female investigator highlights two recurrent features of the crime genre: the first is the perception of women as 'natural victims' and in particular the notion that women who stray beyond the boundaries of accepted female behaviour are somehow deserving of punishment. The second is the exclusion of women from the sphere of knowledge and power, which relegates them to the role of passive agent who must seek protection and justice through men.

In Maud Tabachnik's *Un été pourri* (1994), four men are killed and mutilated but what appears at first to be the work of a serial killer is eventually revealed to be the actions of four distinct killers, each with their own motive. The victims are a child rapist, a man who violently attacks his girlfriend when she refuses to have sex with him in a park, another who tries to rape a woman in an alley and, finally, a man who takes advantage of a crowded tube train to make unwelcome advances to another man. In only the last two cases are the killers directly threatened by their victims and this configuration, together with the multiplicity of the crimes, is crucial: the killers have all experienced events in the past which prompt them to react even when they are only witnesses to the incidents, hence highlighting that the 'crimes' committed by their 'victims', and which remain unpunished by society, are not isolated occurrences but part of a social pattern in which violence against women, and in some cases men, is common. One of those killers is Sandra Kahn, a journalist whose girl-friend was brutally raped and murdered and who finds out that the man she suspects of the crime is on trial for the rape of a ten-year-old girl. When he is acquitted on a technicality, she seeks him out and metes out her own punishment. The character is striking on several levels. Her previous brush with crime (as the partner of a victim) highlights a failure of the justice system: the investigating policemen were more interested in the fact that the rape and murder victim lived with another woman than in securing evidence which would have led to the conviction of the attacker. She also remains unpunished for the murder, as Sam Goodman (the inves-tigating detective, whose name can be seen as more than a coincidence given that he is the only truly sympathetic male character in the novel) comes to see her actions as dictated by moral, if not legal, justice and cannot resign himself to arresting her. This is, of course, a major disrup-tion of the traditional crime narrative in which the killer is unmasked, judged and disposed of so that order may be restored. Finally, and perhaps most surprisingly, Kahn returns in subsequent novels, not as the criminal but as the investigator.

In Andrea H. Japp's *La Raison des femmes* (1999), the killers are a woman and her mother who methodically murder the men who, ten years previously, raped and caused the death of the woman's autistic daughter. As a single woman, a prostitute and the mother of a child whose difficul-ties were seen as a result of a deficient emotional bond between parent and child, the main protagonist feels that the official justice system will not look upon her case favourably and decides to seek vengeance through her own means. Whilst the traditional investigative narrative remains intact, the reader is provoked into sympathizing with the criminal/victim.

Many female writers also make the deliberate choice to subvert the traditional closure of crime narratives. In a society where discrimination and violence against women are still prevalent, there can be no satisfac-tory resolution: the return to order usually provided by the denouement is only a return to a flawed order in which women still struggle to assert and protect themselves. While a specific threat may be removed, it is clear that others lurk. The last scene of Tabachnik's *Gémeaux* (1998), for example, finds Sandra Kahn and her lover at home; unaware they are being observed by one of the serial killing twins pursued by Kahn but who has managed to get away when his brother was shot down and is now bent on revenge.

Feminist fiction?

The fact that we find similarities between authors in terms of characterization and their attempts to subvert or abandon particular features of crime writing certainly seems to suggest that there may be such a genre as French feminist crime fiction. However, it would be a mistake to see this as the sole contribution of female writers to crime fiction. As far as those writers are concerned who are critical of the didactic approach and overtly feminist agenda of their American colleagues' writing, their refusal to be categorized by their gender does not mean that they do not consider themselves 'feminists' in other areas of their lives. Many of them (Japp, Vargas, Tabachnik, Manotti) do claim the label in their 'non-literary' life, a point worth noting given the suspicion generally aroused by the term in France. Nonetheless, we can see that clear contradictions are often apparent between the statement that their fiction is not feminist and the impression produced by the narrative. Perhaps we should simply understand by this that they see feminism as an active position which is suited to militant action rather than literary discussion. It remains, however, that while their work avoids the authorial intrusion often found in American feminist crime fiction, even when the narrative does not directly or overtly relate to women's issues, the society presented, and in particular its gender bias, is implicitly criticized.

When the main character is a woman, the events of her life frequently lead the reader towards a reflection on gender issues, even when neither the author nor the narrator intervene to highlight them. Stylistically, it could be argued that this is in fact far more effective than the 'interventionist' approach, as the reader is not given an opportunity to skip any obviously political aside or to react against a perceptibly didactic strategy. For example, the plot of Japp's *Le Ventre des lucioles* (2001) revolves around the prostitution networks which 'import' women from the former eastern bloc, a phenomenon which intertwines gender with political and economic issues. In a previous volume, her main protagonist, Gloria, has had to decide whether or not she will go through with an abortion. Significantly, although she decides to let the pregnancy run its course, the theme is introduced in such a way that it does not offer any clear 'moral' position but rather exposes the difficulties experienced by women in taking such decisions. Similarly, in Virginie Brac's *Sourire Kabyle* (1992), although the main character's decision to have an abortion is entirely unambiguous, the emotional anguish and social pressures associated with the procedure are brought to the forefront, without being directly linked to the investigation which constitutes the main interest of the narrative.

The emphasis on social issues goes some way to explain why most French female writers shun the *roman à énigme* (mystery novel), often presented as the preserve of women because of its lack of overt violence, in favour of the more gritty *noir*. Of course, the mention of *noir* immediately brings to mind images of a Humphrey Bogart-like, hard-drinking, womanizing 'private dick', the very term a suggestion that this is male territory. We may wonder, therefore, in what ways female writers have altered that definition. Like the traditional 'private eye', female investigators are often reluctantly drawn to investigate by circumstances rather than choice (although, unlike him, they tend to have a personal interest in the inquiry) and what we are given to see of their private lives is frequently dismal. Japp's main character, Gloria Parker-Simmons, a brilliant scientist often called to the rescue by the FBI, was abused by her father and consequently gave birth to a disabled daughter. Isolated by her genius and her inability to form relationships, on several occasions in the course of five volumes she is to be found passed out on the floor of her flat from alcohol abuse. Tabachnik's recurrent heroine, Sandra Kahn, seems even more marginal: in the first volume she is herself pursued by the police for murdering the man who raped and killed her lover. By the second volume she has come to an uneasy understanding with her former pursuer, police officer Sam Goodman, and oscillates between helping him in his work and taking centre stage in her own investigations. Despite this tentative alliance with an official authority figure, a lesbian journalist who relies on Prozac to get through the day seems a far cry from Miss Marple. In other words, they are typical *noir* anti-heroes, solitary avengers rather than detectives. As such, they fit the traditional mould, but with one essential difference. If we accept, as posited by Reuter, that the basis of traditional male characterization is 'the conflict between the values of some heroes (most notably private eyes) and a decaying world in which such values have been lost',[11] then an important distinction must be made: contemporary female characters do not long for a lost paradise, they do not rely on an outdated but 'superior' set of values or code of behaviour. Rather, they are engaged in resisting long-established values as far as gender is concerned. The order which was the private eye's lost paradise is their nightmare and those they hunt and are in turn hunted by are the products of it. What they are seeking is not a return to old values but, rather, the establishment of a new set of values, a world where they would not be harmed. The authors use the crime narrative both to expose the way in which women are treated by society and to debunk some old-fashioned myths about the 'nature' of women. The figure of the avenger is ideally suited to challenge the notion that women are less violent than men and therefore features frequently in crime narratives by women. In an ironic twist, the assumption that women shun, or are unable to resort to, violence often slows down the enquiry of both the 'official' detectives who pursue the avenger and the amateur investigator, as they are unable to accept the possibility of a brutal crime being the work of a woman.[12]

It must be noted, however, that while violence often underpins narratives it is neither the main point of interest nor, in most cases, voyeuristic. Our attention is drawn instead to its aftermath and, rather than to the work of professional detectives on the inquiry, to the victim's viewpoint or to the impact of crime on those left behind. Poole's remark about Vargas that:

> men and women, old and young, rich and poor die, all of them despatched speedily (these are not gory novels) by the cruel or the desperate, many of them leaving a sorrowing entourage whose despair is never glossed over – unusually for the genre, the legacy of murder is much emphasized[13]

could easily be applied to many of Vargas's contemporaries. In her series, the lasting consequences of violence are exposed and characters carry the physical and emotional scars of the violence they have experienced or witnessed from one book to the next. This has been identified as one of the innovations of contemporary crime fiction by women in France, one of the ways in which they have 'renewed' the genre, but this analysis should come with some reservations: while perhaps more frequent in recent writing by women, it is neither new (Mary R. Rhinehart, mentioned earlier, is credited with introducing an emphasis on the psychology of the victim in the early twentieth century) nor the preserve of women writers. Both Jean Amila, with *Le Boucher des hurlus* (1981), and Sébastien Japrisot, with *L'Été meurtrier* (*One Deadly Summer*, 1978), focus their narratives on the victim's perception of crime and their desire for revenge. Similar precedents can be found for the authors' reluctance to provide neat closure. As Reuter points out: 'As for the neat ending of the whodunnit, it rarely exists in *noir* writing, in which the plot is often extremely complex and the outcome frequently ambiguous, leaving many issues unresolved.'[14]

The only conclusion which can therefore be drawn with some degree of certainty is not that women are so much changing the *noir* novel, but that the genre attracts female writers because of its focus on social issues and on the figure of the outsider, albeit with a shift in ideology where the latter is concerned, and because of its refusal to see crime as an anomaly in society rather than as a natural result of its flawed moral code. Yet the vision of society that female crime writers offer is not solely negative. For one thing it reflects the progress made by French women in the workplace. Brigitte Aubert, Noëlle Loriot and Hélène de Monaghan all represent female judges in their novels; Michèle Rozenfarb and Danielle Thiéry feature female *commissaires*, to name but a few. Such characters may have been unthinkable fifty years ago but they are rooted in today's reality. Sue Neale's assertion that '[French female crime writers] have often found it necessary to set their narratives in America rather than in France, thereby skirting the issue of the implausibility of French women in high ranking positions in the police'[15] must therefore be tempered by the authors' own, rather more positive, perception of bridging the gender divide in French society and by some concrete evidence of progress. The first four female police superintendents were appointed in 1975, the first Lieutenant de Gendarmerie Mobile (motorized army police lieutenant) in 1989, while Martine Monteil started at the head of the Brigade Criminelle (crime squad), the most prestigious department of the French police, in 1996 and is now director of the Police Judiciaire (CID). Both Granotier and Manotti have in fact pointed out in interviews that the presence of women in crime writing seems to be linked, chronologically, to the appointment of a growing number of women as judges, high-ranking police officers and Cabinet ministers.

Beyond gender

While it may be true that particular trends can be seen to recur in some women crime writers' work, it cannot be said to be true of all of them or to constitute a particular genre since they may also be found in male writers' work. Furthermore, some female writers stand out in that it has been assumed, at least at the beginning of their careers, that they were male. It is certainly not by coincidence that two of the most successful contemporary female crime writers write under gender-ambiguous pseudonyms, Dominique Manotti and Fred Vargas. However, unlike their predecessors, who found it necessary to hide behind male pseudonyms in order to get published, their decision to use such *noms de plume* comes as a reaction to the purely artificial notion of a *polar féminin* and from a desire to be judged on the quality of their work as part of a wider field than that of women writers. In other words, they use them to attempt to avoid triggering any preconceptions the reader may have when seeing a female name on the cover of a book.

Dominique Manotti cites James Ellroy as her main influence and sees her work as *témoignage*, a witness account of a particular time in history, a snapshot of society, its flaws and its struggles. Manotti's *engagement* (political commitment) as a unionist is clearly reflected in her fiction. In fact, it was her stint as a union organizer in the Paris sweatshops of the clothing industry which prompted her to write her first book, *Sombre sentier* (*Rough Trade*, 1995), as a means of exposing the exploitation of illegal immigrants. Later works have all aimed to put the spotlight, through crime writing, on the financial and political machinations of the higher echelons of French society. *Nos fantastiques années fric* (2001) throws light on the wheeling and dealing of the later years of the Mitterrand administration, while *Kop* (1998) denounces the way in which political parties are financed and *Lorraine connection* (2006) reveals the corruption and human cost of the sale of one of France's largest companies. This emphasis on political issues in the narrower sense of the term makes Manotti's work far more akin to that of male writers such as Didier Daeninckx or Jean-Hugues Oppel than to that of any of her female contemporaries.

Similarly, Fred Vargas is often seen as being in a class of her own. She stands apart from her contemporaries, both male and female, in terms of both style and purpose. Her writing is poetic, often verging on the fantastical (the hunt for a werewolf in *Seeking Whom He May Devour* or the overnight appearance of a fully grown beech tree in *The Three Evangelists*). Vargas has stated on many occasions that she sees the crime novel, or *Rompol* as she prefers to call it, as 'modern myth', based on clear notions of good and evil. Her narratives follow a pattern of transgression–explanation–catharsis similar to that found in classical tragedy. She argues that her work addresses anxieties which are not social but existential.[16] It is true that, 'while it is undeniable that many social concerns, situating the narrative firmly in the France of the 90s, are raised in Vargas's work, these are nowhere made into causes (nor indeed into motives: poverty, unemployment, etc. may be present and indeed have a high profile, but they inspire none of the plentiful murders whose investigation shapes the plots)'.[17]

So while Danglard, a police inspector who brings up the five children left behind by his wife (and who are not all his), experiences the difficulties of single parenthood, or Camille and Soliman are confronted with racism in *Seeking Whom He May Devour*, those references to social issues are present simply as part of modern life in France. They are, in fact, part of the realistic (but not 'realist') tenor of the narrative. The main objective for Vargas is not to highlight these issues but to raise and then relieve the reader's existential anxieties by presenting and then explaining the extraordinary. This is done in part through emblematic figures who can, much as the scapegoat of ancient tragedy, shoulder the burden of evil and whose capture or destruction ensures a return to a 'safe' order.[18] It is no surprise therefore to find that, unlike many of her contemporaries, Vargas insist that closure is an integral and necessary part of the crime novel.

This fidelity to a fairly traditional form is also found in other features of her work. So despite the recurrent and problematic relationship between Adamsberg and Camille, Vargas insists that love should not appear prominently in the crime novel and the traditional tools of detection are in evidence (nail clippings provide a crucial clue in *Seeking Whom He May Devour*, for example).[19] Yet this apparent conventionality is mitigated by surreal events and unconventional characters. Adamsberg, the most frequently recurrent of Vargas's characters, is far from relying on the scientific precision of a Sherlock Holmes. Intuitive rather than logical, he is described as 'slow', infuriates his colleagues with his apparent irrationality and is more likely to reach the solution to the enigma through some mysterious epiphany on one of his aimless perambulations along the Seine than through logical deduction. In the extract below, there is no explanation offered for Adamsberg's conviction that despite the fact that such signs have historically been designed to protect (as the rational Danglard points out), the 'tagger' who has been painting numbers on doors is 'not into saving souls. He's predicting. He's planning. One thing after another. He's setting it all up. He could go into action tomorrow. Or tonight.' Yet his instinct will prove to be correct. This reliance on an almost animalistic sixth sense is often associated with vocabulary and metaphors that place Adamberg in the realm of nature and apart from his fellow investigators who, like Danglard, only trust rational and scientific methods. The image of the 'acetylene flame' and the glow that accompanies Adamsberg's 'supernatural' deductions give him an almost religious aura. He is a seer rather than an investigator and therefore an oddity in the world of the detective novel, a world in which the investigator is traditionally remote, neutral and concerned only with the facts.

This chapter has shown that, while it is tempting to extract from the body of evidence some generalities about women crime writers, to do so is, to some extent, tantamount to dismissing the wide variety of genres within crime writing and women's contributions to each of them, as well as the unique qualities of individual authors. Whilst some features foreground women and their concerns or suggest a world-view which is affected by gender, it cannot be argued that this limits the scope of these writers' concerns. The notion of global conspiracies, the corrupting influence of money in politics and the threat of a new world order, either for personal gain or religious reasons, are evident in the works of Tabachnik (*Les Cercles de l'enfer*, 2004; *L'Empreinte du nain*, 1999) and Stéphanie Benson (*Cavalier seul*, 2001), whilst a deep disillusion with the ethics of the French political scene forms the basis of Manotti's writing. Tabachnik is noted for a number of crime novels which take as their focal point the collaboration of French citizens with the Nazis during the Second World War and its consequences for the next generation, above all anti-Semitism (*La Honte leur appartient*, 2002; *La Mémoire du bourreau*, 2001; *Le Tango des assassins*, 2002). Dominique Manotti also puts French collaboration at the heart of her novel *Le Corps noir* (2004). It is worth noting that, regardless of the gender of the author, such concerns with the less honourable areas of French history are reminiscent of the thematic of key 1980s *néo-polar* novels, such as Didier Daeninckx's *Meurtres pour mémoire* (*Murder in Memoriam*, 1984). In addition, the writers themselves are keen to claim their individuality and many have attempted to set the record straight by pointing out both the perennial presence of women in crime writing and the fact that there is no such thing as *le polar féminin* but rather crime fiction, in various sub-genres and of varying quality, which happens to be written by women. Indeed, this analysis of crime narratives by women in the twentieth and early twenty-first centuries makes it clear that their contribution to crime fiction has been abundant, varied and innovative. They have produced works of note in every genre, applying, subverting and challenging rules, and brought new preoccupations and dimensions to a field long ridden with clichés and perceived as a lesser form of literature. It is clear then that, while female writers may have been the forgotten protagonists of the history of crime writing in the past, they can no longer be ignored and will undoubtedly have to be counted upon in future.

* * *

Extract from Fred Vargas's *Have Mercy on Us All*

Joss, a disgraced sailor, has revived the profession of town crier in the Paris district of Montparnasse, where people pay him to read out their news, job offers and items for sale or declarations of love. Recently, his message box has been filled daily with extracts from books, all predicting a mysterious calamity. Meanwhile, someone has been painting a strange sign on doors during the night. New signs are appearing every night and commissaire Adamsberg, aided by Inspector Danglard, is investigating.

Adamsberg put one hand on his desk to steady himself and looked down at the floor with the fax hanging from his other hand. So the reverse 4 was a charm against the plague. Thirty-odd blocks daubed with the sign, and a whole stack of messages in the town crier's inbox. Tomorrow, the Londoner of 1665 was going to see his first corpse. With furrowed brow Adamsberg plodded through the decorator's rubbish and into Danglard's office.

'Danglard, your radical art fellow is behaving like a real idiot.'

Adamsberg put the fax in front of his deputy, who read it with suspicion. Then he reread it.

'Hmm. Now I remember. I saw that shape in the wrought-iron balustrade of the magistrates' court at Nancy. A historic monument, that building was. There were two 4s together, one the right way round, the other backwards way on, just like that.'

'So what do we do with your subversive installation artist, Danglard?'

'I've already told you. We put him on the back burner.'

'And then what?'

'We bring in someone else. A crackpot apostle who reckons he's saving his brothers and sisters from the plague.'

'No, he's not into saving souls. He's predicting. He's planning. One thing after another. He's setting it all up. He could go into action tomorrow. Or tonight.'

Danglard had become expert in reading Adamsberg's face. It could pass without transition from looking as cold as a rained-out bonfire to the intensity of an acetylene flame. When that happened, some still unexplained physiological process made Adamsberg's swarthy skin glow. Danglard knew from long experience that it would be pointless to contradict the man, to express any kind of doubt or to point out logical flaws in his position. All objections would just turn to steam, like drips falling on hot coals. So he preferred to keep his doubts bottled up and to save them for a less heated moment. At the same time Adamsberg's moments of intensity brought Danglard up against his own contradictions. The chief's passionate intuitions cut Danglard adrift from his rational moorings, yet he had to admit that he found it oddly relaxing to throw caution and common sense to the winds.

Fred Vargas, *Have Mercy on Us All* (2001), trans. David Bellos (London: Vintage, 2004), pp. 94–5.

Notes

[1] Deborah Hamilton, 'The French detective fiction novel 1920's–1990's: gendering a genre' (unpublished Ph.D. thesis, Pennsylvania State University, 1994), 18.

[2] Michel Amelin, 'Celles qui assassinèrent', *Enigmatika*, 36 (1989), 11–20 (20).

[3] 'La brutalité et l'érotisme ont remplacé les savantes déductions. Le détective ne ramasse plus de cendres de cigarette, mais écrase le nez des témoins à coups de talon. Les bandits sont parfaitement immondes, sadiques et lâches, et toutes les femmes ont des jambes splendides; elles sont perfides et traîtresses et non moins cruelles que les messieurs.' *http://www.gallimard.fr/collections/serie_noire.htm.*

[4] Amelin, 'Celles qui assassinèrent', 17.

[5] 'De multiples débats se déroulent entre hommes, sur les liens entre cinéma et polar, sur l'esthétique, le style, la sociologie, etc … du polar, tandis que nous débattons inlassablement des femmes et du polar … C'est … une façon de nous renvoyer à l'éternel féminin.' Dominique Manotti, 'Chéries noires', *La Raison présente*, 134 (2000), 91–6 (94).

[6] D. E. Hamilton, 'Genre, gender and politics in French detective fiction of the 1930s: Camille Hedwige's *L'Appel de la morte*', *Forum for Modern Language Studies*, 24/1 (1998), 56–67 (59).

[7] Ibid., 64.

[8] Ibid., 66.

[9] S. Noreiko, 'Toutes des salopes: representations of women in French crime fiction', *French Cultural Studies*, 10 (1999), 89–105 (96).

[10] Interview with Fred Vargas, Paris, March 2000.

[11] '[L]e conflit entre les valeurs de certains héros (notamment les privés) et un monde "dégradé", dans lequel les valeurs se sont perdues', Yves Reuter, *Le Roman policier* (Paris: Nathan, 1997), p. 61.

[12] See, for example, Japp, *La Raison des femmes*, in which the main investigator's mission is impeded, as much as anything, by his rookie colleague's inability to factor in the possibility that the killer may be a woman (pp. 178–9), In Tabachnik's *Un été pourri*, one of the investigators exclaims: 'This is not a woman's crime …' (p. 63). In Aubert's *La Mort des bois*, the notion that the killer might be a woman does not occur to any of the protagonists until the evidence prohibits any other possibility.

[13] S. Poole, 'Rompols not of the Bailey: Fred Vargas and the polar as mini-proto-mythe', *French Cultural Studies*, 12 (2001), 95–108 (107).

[14] 'Quant à la clarté finale du roman à énigme, elle n'existe que très rarement dans le roman noir, aux intrigues souvent fort complexes et à l'issue fréquemment ambiguë, laissant de larges zones d'ombre, derrière elle ou dans l'avenir'. Reuter, *Le Roman policer*, p. 66. He cites as examples Hammett's *The Maltese Falcon*, Chandler's *The Big Sleep* and Himes's *Blind Man with a Pistol*.

[15] See *http://www.crimeculture.com/Contents/FrenchCrimeFiction.htm.*

[16] 'Ce n'est pas la remise en ordre du chaos, enfin de la peur du désordre social. C'est la peur du désordre interne, c'est la peur de mourir.' (It is not about fighting chaos, that is to say social disorder. It's about internal chaos, about the fear of death.) Interview with Fred Vargas, Paris, March 2000.

[17] Poole, 'Rompols not of the Bailey', 99.

104

18 'Je crois que le roman policier est en effet l'héritier de la catharsis grecque, de la tragédie antique, de la fatalité, qui s'élabore à partir d'une transgression … c'est une mise en scène d'une transgression, d'une tension, d'une projection des problèmes du public sur ce théâtre, problèmes les plus profonds …' (I do believe that the crime novel is the modern incarnation of Greek catharsis, of ancient tragedy, which arises from a transgression. It is the staging of a transgression, of a tension, it is putting the audience's most intimate troubles on the stage …) Interview with Fred Vargas, Paris, March 2000.

19 'Qu'une histoire sentimentale soit au centre d'un roman policier pour moi est un contresens. Pour ma vision du roman policier.' (In my eyes, for a sentimental tale to be at the heart of a crime novel is a misinterpretation of the genre.) Interview with Fred Vargas, Paris, March 2000.

Select bibliography

Arley, Catherine, *Le Talion* (Paris: Interpress, 1967).

Aubert, Brigitte, *La Mort des bois* (Paris: Seuil, 1996). *Death from the Woods*, trans. David L. Koral (New York: Berkley Prime Crime, 2005).

——, *La Mort des neiges* (Paris: Seuil, 2000). *Death from the Snows*, trans. David L. Koral (New York: Welcome Rain, 2005).

Brac, Virginie, *Tropique du pervers* (Paris: Fleuve Noir, 2000).

——, *Double peine* (Paris: Fleuve Noir, 2004).

Fonteneau, Pascale, *Confidences sur l'escalier* (Paris: Gallimard, 1992).

——, *États de lame* (Paris: Gallimard, 1993).

Granotier, Sylvie, *Sueurs chaudes* (Paris: Gallimard, 1997).

——, *Dodo* (Paris: Gallimard, 2000).

Hanska, Evane, *La Raison du plus mort* (Paris: Flammarion, 1999).

Japp, Andrea H., *La Bostonienne* (Paris: Librairie des Champs-Élysées, 1991).

——, *La Femelle de l'espèce* (Paris: Librairie des Champs-Élysées, 1996).

——, *La Raison des femmes* (Paris: Librairie des Champs-Élysées, 1999).

Loriot, Noëlle, *L'Inculpé* (Paris: Albin Michel, 1991).

——, *Meurtrière bourgeoisie* (Paris: Albin Michel, 2004).

Manotti, Dominique, *Sombre sentier* (Paris: Seuil: 1995). *Rough Trade*, trans. Margaret Crosland and Elfreda Powell (London: Arcadia Books, 2006).

——, *A vos chevaux* (Paris: Rivages, 1997). *Dead Horse Meat*, trans. Amanda Hopkinson and Ros Schwartz (London: Arcadia Books, 2006).

——, *Kop* (Paris: Rivages, 1998).

——, *Nos fantastiques années fric* (Paris: Rivages, 2001).

——, *Le Corps noir* (Paris: Seuil, 2004).

——, *Lorraine connection* (Paris: Rivages, 2006).

Monaghan, Hélène de, *Esprit de suite* (Paris: Librairie des Champs-Élysées, 1972).

——, *Vacances éternelles* (Paris: Librairie des Champs-Élysées, 1974).

——, *Le Couperet* (Paris: Denoël, 1987).

Oriano, Janine, *B comme Baptiste* (Paris: Gallimard, 1971).

Pelletier, Chantal, *Le Chant du bouc* (Paris: Gallimard, 2000). *Goat Song*, trans. Ian Monk (London: Bitter Lemon Press, 2004).

——, *Eros et Thalasso* (Paris: Gallimard, 1998).

Rozenfarb, Michèle, *Chapeau!* (Paris: Gallimard: 1998).

Saint André, Alix de, *L'Ange et le réservoir de liquide à freins* (Paris: Gallimard, 1994).

Soulas, Antoinette, *Mort d'une ombre* (Paris: Librairie des Champs-Élysées, 1958).

Sylvain, Dominique, *Baka!* (Paris: Viviane Hamy, 1995).

——, *Passage du désir* (Paris: Viviane Hamy, 2004).

——, *Manta corridor* (Paris: Viviane Hamy, 2006).

Tabachnik, Maud, *Un été pourri* (Paris: Viviane Hamy, 1994).

——, *Gémeaux* (Paris: Viviane Hamy, 1998).

Thiéry, Danielle, *Mises à mort* (Paris: Robert Laffont, 1998).

Vargas, Fred, *Pars vite et reviens tard* (Paris: Viviane Hamy, 2001). *Have Mercy on Us All*, trans. David Bellos (London: Vintage, 2004).

——, *L'Homme à l'envers* (Paris: Vivane Hamy, 1999). *Seeking Whom He May Devour*, trans. David Bellos (London: Vintage, 2006).

——, *Debout les morts* (Paris: Viviane Hamy, 1995). *The Three Evangelists*, trans. Siân Reynolds (London: Harvill Secker, 2006).

——, *Sous les vents de Neptune* (Paris: Viviane Hamy, 2004). *Wash This Blood Clean from my Hand*, trans. Siân Reynolds (London: Harvill Secker, 2007).

Further secondary reading

Desnain, Véronique, 'Elise ou la vraie vie? Reality and fiction in Brigitte Aubert', *Modern and Contemporary France*, 12 (2004), 199–211.

——, 'La femelle de l'espèce: women in contemporary French crime fiction', *French Cultural Studies*, 12 (2001), 175–92.

——, 'Female crime writers in contemporary France', *Arachnofile* (University of Edinburgh's SELC Electronic Journal), 1 (2000), *www.selc.ed.ac.uk/arach-nofiles/pages/one_desnain_main.htm.*

Gorrara, Claire, 'Feminist fictions: Maud Tabachnik's *Un été pourri* (1994)', *The Roman Noir in Post-War French Culture* (Oxford: Oxford University Press, 2003), pp. 107–23.

Neale, Sue, 'Contemporary French crime fiction – a search for the hidden with particular reference to *Sous les vents de Neptune* by Fred Vargas', *www. extra.rdg.ac.uk/2001group/Articles-studyDay/Vargas%20(Sue%20Neale).pdf.*

www.polarféminin.com is a useful web-based resource, although many of the authors presented are British or American.

6

Postmodern Detectives and French Traditions

SIMON KEMP

Postmodernism

The term *postmodern* has been applied to many areas of western culture of the last half century – architecture and the visual arts, literature and film, philosophy and critical theory – often to things which might seem to have little in common with one another. In order to work out what a postmodern detective story may be, we ought perhaps to begin by looking briefly at what is characteristic to the postmodern itself. In postmodern art, we think of Andy Warhol's paintings of soup cans and silk-screen prints of Marilyn Monroe or Roy Lichtenstein's blow-ups of cheaply printed comic strips. In architecture there is Paris's Pompidou Centre with its brightly coloured ducting exposed on the outside of the building or the eccentric silver curves and humps of Bilbao's Guggenheim Museum. Postmodern litera-ture includes John Fowles's *The French Lieutenant's Woman* (1969) and Kurt Vonnegut's *Slaughterhouse Five* (1969), both of which play subver-sive games with familiar literary genres (nineteenth-century realism in the former and science fiction in the latter), while self-consciously putting the writing process at the forefront of the story. In the cinema we have Ridley Scott's *Blade Runner* (1982) or David Lynch's *Blue Velvet* (1986), which also take an irreverent approach to a familiar genre, in this case the classic *film noir*, which Scott merges with science fiction to investigate what it means to be human, and which Lynch pushes to the boundaries of surreal nightmare. And in postmodern thought, often linked to the theorists of post-structuralism, Jean-François Lyotard's 'postmodern condition' sees our era as characterized by a collapse of faith in great systems which purported to explain the world; Jean Baudrillard's simulacra suggest a culture in which copies have supplanted their originals and Jacques Derrida's deconstruction puts established ideas in question by searching out their internal contradictions, hidden assumptions and the indeter-minacy of their language.[1]

One recurrent factor in these examples is an engagement with what already exists, rather than an attempt to be entirely new. Umberto Eco, discussing his own postmodern crime novel, *The Name of the Rose* (1980), has suggested that postmodernism arose from a recognition that the modernist drive to break with the past in search of ever new forms had exhausted itself, and in its place came cultural forms that revisited the past 'but with irony, not innocently'.[2] A Lichtenstein painting offers different pleasures from a comic strip, and Lynch treats his *noir* material very differently from, say, Howard Hawks in *The Big Sleep* (1946). Both Lichtenstein and Lynch, however, require from the viewer some degree of familiarity with their source genres if we are to appreciate how they have transformed their models. Another element we see in common is *play*, itself a key term in post-structuralist thought. Postmodern architecture plays with the conventions and possibilities of building; postmodern novels exhibit a playful engagement with the traditions of novel writing. Where this playfulness combines with revisiting the past, what results is a pastiche of pre-existing forms. For Fredric Jameson, a generally hostile commentator on postmodernism, pastiche is its defining art form, producing ironic re-imaginings of old images and ideas, now largely devoid of personal expression or emotional impact.[3] Playing with the cultural past also affords an opportunity for critique: in fiction particularly, postmodern pastiche can act as a commentary on its target genre, laying bare the rules of its construction and the ideology behind its value judgements. It is an opportunity that Fowles, Vonnegut and Eco all take up, and this kind of fiction about fiction (sometimes called metafiction) is widespread in literature of the period. Lastly, we see in many of these examples an interest in popular culture – in consumer items, film stars, comic strips and pulp genres; although whether this represents an egalitarian breakdown of divisions between 'high' and 'low' culture, or an elitist condescension to the 'raw materials' with which they work, is an open question.

We already get an inkling of why crime fiction should play a major role in French postmodernism. It offers well-defined formulas which are ripe for mimicry, with plot, character roles and archetypal milieux being widely familiar to French readers. Its typical narrative structure is sufficiently predictable for the postmodernist to play games with readers' expectations, and the genre already contains a strong element of metafiction in its tradition of the detective- or sidekick-narrator commenting on his/her reconstruction of the story of the crime. Even where the detective story differs most sharply from postmodern trends, in its unshakeable faith in the power of truth and reason which seems far from the sceptical relativism of much postmodern thought, it offers scope for subversive play that might question such a philosophy. Let us see how far these potentialities are borne out in practice.

The OuLiPo group

While precursors of postmodern crime fiction can be seen in early twentieth-century literature, for instance in surrealist poet Robert Desnos's refashioning of the pulp Fantômas mysteries into an epic twenty-six-stanza poem, 'La Complainte de Fantômas' (1933), we begin in earnest with Raymond Queneau's *Pierrot mon ami* (1942), which has all the ingredients of a detective story (and much else besides), but unfortunately not assembled in the right order. The narrator ruefully comments in the epilogue:

> He saw the novel that all this could have made, a crime novel with a murder, a culprit and a detective, and … he saw the novel that it had made, a novel so devoid of cleverness that it was not even possible to know if there was a puzzle to be solved in it or not, a novel in which everything could have linked up in detective-story style, but which was in reality entirely lacking in the pleasures afforded by a spectacle or activity of this kind.[4]

The deliberate malfunctioning of the crime fiction plot draws the reader's attention to the genre's hidden artifice: the puzzle must, for instance, be solved by a series of logical steps with each clue leading to the next or the narrative will have no development; retrospective narrators must conceal their hindsight from the reader if they are not to short-circuit the plot by revealing too much too soon. Sabotaging crime fiction's conventions to show up their contingency is a common strategy in postmodern detective stories, and is very much in evidence in the work of the international writers' group that Queneau was later to help found, OuLiPo (Ouvroir de littérature potentielle) (the Workshop of Potential Literature).

The writers of the OuLiPo group, founded in 1960 and still in existence today, were brought together by a shared interest in rules, often mathematical or linguistic, which could be brought to bear on their literary work as a spur to creativity. Georges Perec produced perhaps the best-known examples of this with his two 'lipogrammatic' novels, *La Disparition* (*A Void*, 1969) and *Les Revenentes* (*The Exeter Text*, 1972), the first of which has no letter 'e' in the text, and second of which has no other vowels but 'e'. Both novels are to a large extent crime fiction pastiche, the former in an especially interesting way, since the mystery to be investigated is the disappearance of the letter 'e' from the world of the story. The 'rules' of the crime novel, which various crime writers have made doomed attempts to codify through the genre's history, hold obvious attractions for these writers, and both Perec and another OuLiPo writer, Jacques Roubaud, have maintained a consistent interest in the genre through their careers. Roubaud's *La Belle Hortense* (1985) and its two sequels have fun with the conventions of the form, as narrator, 'author' and 'reader' squabble over the telling of a tale in which the characters are quite aware that they are in a detective story and aware of what this implies about the way events ought to unfold. The detective criticizes the mystery for its lack of a murder. At the denouement, he is prevented from recapping the story so far, for fear of sending the narrative into an endless loop which would prevent it reaching the moment of the criminal's arrest. And a description of the detective's office bears an uncanny similarity to a 1920s Maigret novel, sparking a row about plagiarism between 'author' and narrator. Perec too sabotages his own crime fiction for comic effect. His master-piece, *La Vie mode d'emploi* (*Life, A User's Manual*, 1978) contains several parodic detective stories among its cornucopia of narratives, each attached to one of the rooms or inhabitants of a Paris apartment building. The stories are reminiscent of the schematic puzzle-plots of Agatha Christie, of whom Perec was an admirer, but pushed to ludicrous extremes. One mystery has a crime scene filled with all manner of exotic clues, another has no evidence at all. In one story the culprit turns out to be none of the suspects, in another, all of the suspects, plus the suicidal victim himself, are revealed to have made coincidentally simultaneous attempts on the victim's life.[5] As with Roubaud, the point of the exercise is laughter, but in both cases there is implied critique in the comedy of a genre that strains plausibility in search of the perfect mystery, but finds its own arti-fice something of an embarrassment. More sustained and serious engagement with crime fiction comes in Perec's *'53 jours'* (*'53 Days'*, 1989), sadly left unfinished and published posthumously. This ingenious work begins with a series of nested detective stories in each of which the vital clue to the mystery lies in a crime novel found at the scene. Readers are led down through successive levels of narrative, accompanied by detectives who are reading alongside us, commenting on the workings of each story as we go. Perec thus combines some accomplished crime fiction with a metafictional exploration of the form, exposing the intricate formulas of the mystery plot, before we discover, at the heart of all the stories, a certain 'G.P.' who has masterminded the whole business.

The 'New Novel'

Along with OuLiPo, the other major experimental movement in post-modern French literature is the loosely connected group of writers known as the *nouveaux romanciers*, or New Novelists. In the 1950s, the Minuit publishing house became home to a number of writers, including Alain Robbe-Grillet, Nathalie Sarraute, Claude Simon and Michel Butor, who in various ways sought to reinvent the novel, reacting against traditional realism for its 'fraudulent' representation of character or of the physical world, and supplementing their fictional output with polemical essays calling for the literary representation of reality to be rethought. Once again, metafictional concerns find a useful proving ground in crime fiction, where the tensions between the requirements of the puzzle-plot and of realism can be unpicked and examined, and where the genre's naturally questioning tone and self-conscious narration can be exploited for an investigation into representation itself. Crime themes are touched upon in many New Novels, among them Robert Pinget's *L'Inquisitoire* (*The Interview Room*, 1962) or Simon's *Le Vent* (*The Wind*, 1975), but probably the most interesting encounters with the genre come from Butor's *L'Emploi du temps* (*Passing Time*, 1956) and Robbe-Grillet's *Les Gommes* (*The Erasers*, 1953). *L'Emploi du temps* takes the form of a diary written by a young Frenchman, Jacques Revel, during a year in the fictional British city of Bleston, based largely on Manchester. When Revel's acquaintance, the crime novelist George Burton, is knocked down in a hit-and-run accident, Revel becomes convinced that it was attempted murder, motivated by what he takes to be references to a real unsolved crime in Burton's novel, *Le Meurtre de Bleston* (*Bleston Murder*). However, both the form that Revel's account of his investigation takes and its eventual conclusion mark *L'Emploi du temps* out as quite different from conventional crime fiction. The novel begins straightforwardly as Revel recalls, in May, the events of his arrival the previous October. However, with each passing month of writing, Revel adds a new narrative strand to his journal, weaving together accounts of the present and the past and narrating his own re-reading of the diary, so that by September his diary is skipping between five different timelines, two of which run backwards. This immensely complex structure, through which Revel tries to connect events from different points of time in Bleston and to link the supposed crime back to the incidents which provoked it, is compared in the novel itself to the structure of the detective story. In a lecture on the art of the crime novel by Burton, which Revel records, emphasis is laid on the multi-stranded nature of crime fiction narrative, due to the coexistence within the same text of the story of events leading to the crime and the story of the investigation which follows it. Burton stresses the 'backwards' nature of the crime story as it appears in the text, since it is pieced together by the investigator working from effect to cause. *L'Emploi du temps* is an important example of postmodern crime fiction, partly due to the influence Burton's lecture has had on the theory of the genre, in particular inspiring Tzvetan Todorov's 'A typology of detective fiction'.[6] It is also significant in that its intricate narrative form is itself a pastiche of crime fiction technique, yet it takes a celebratory rather than a hostile attitude to its model. The postmodernists are as keen to make use of crime fiction's unique qualities for the purposes of literary innovation as they are to make fun of its shortcomings to score critical points. The neutral, conflicting or even undecidable standpoint of pastiche with regard to its target is a further hallmark of postmodernism, marking a change from the usually clearly satirical attitude of parody in earlier literary generations.

For all its artistic accomplishment, the investigation diary of *L'Emploi du temps* is, from Revel's point of view, a failure, as he loses himself in a mass of ever accumulating cross-references and gradually obscures the facts beneath distorting layers of hindsight. Finally, as in Queneau's novel, he doubts whether there was a mystery to be solved at all. Such a pessimistic view of the detective's power to uncover truth and restore order is also common in postmodern crime fiction, echoing the scepticism of post-structuralist thought, and it is equally evident in Robbe-Grillet's *Les Gommes*. This novel splices a Simenon-style police procedural with a parodic retelling of the Oedipus story. Its hapless detective, Wallas, spends much of the book going literally and figuratively around in circles as he tries to solve an apparent murder in which all the clues coincidentally point to him as the culprit. The circles close when, twenty-four hours after the crime, Wallas lies in wait for the 'murderer' to return to the scene. On his arrival, Wallas shoots the man dead, only to discover that it is in fact the 'victim' returning home from where he had been hiding out following the failure of the earlier attempt to assassinate him. Despite its clever plot, *Les Gommes* keeps its distance from the traditional pleasures of crime fiction. The true situation is known to the reader from early in the novel and so it is with no mystery and little suspense that we watch Wallas misconstrue sly classical omens as he stumbles towards his appointment with fate. Equally, the novel does not try to accommodate its twist ending within a plausible narrative environment, but instead takes every opportunity to highlight its artificiality, mirroring the scenes of the failed assassination and accidental shooting to a preposterous degree, and including such gratuitous devices as having the detective's watch stop at the moment of the first shooting to restart precisely twenty-four hours on, at the second one. The incompatible logics of Greek tragedy and urban *noir* undermine one another to comic effect, but the outcome is a despondent one, showing a detective whose reason has failed to lead him to the truth, and whose actions have caused only further harm.

This pessimism continues and increases in Robbe-Grillet's later forays into the worlds of crime fiction, as all order breaks down and it begins to seem that we can know nothing at all with any certainty. In *La Maison de rendez-vous* (*The House of Assignation*, 1965) attempts to get to the bottom of the killing of shady Hong Kong businessman, Edouard Manneret, are linked to the trafficking of drugs and women at the Villa Bleue. Helpfully for the reader, the narrator offers us what appears to be an eye-witness account of Manneret's death, killed by a huge black dog which is defending its mistress from his unwelcome advances. Unfortunately, a hundred pages later the narrator offers us a second account, again apparently eye-witness, in which Manneret is shot dead by a certain Ralph Johnson for refusing to lend him money. Between these scenes it is asserted that Manneret is stabbed by a policeman or assassinated by communists. More disconcertingly still, at the same time the Villa Bleue's private theatre is staging a production of *L'Assassinat d'Edouard Manneret* (*The Murder of Edouard Manneret*), the account of which merges into that of the 'real-life' action. The narrator himself is also a problematic figure. He begins with pretensions to classic detective-story precision: 'I shall now attempt, therefore, to recount that evening at Lady Ava's, at any rate to note exactly what were, to my knowledge, the principal events that marked it. I arrived at the Villa Bleue around ten past nine, by taxi.'[7]

However, as the chronology of the tale twists into chaos, it is this single point of certainty to which he helplessly returns, at one point even substituting Johnson for himself as he does so. His claims are put in question as he contradicts himself in the space of a sentence, speculates fruitlessly on matters he has previously asserted as fact and slips between levels of fictionality without warning. At some points it appears he is not even in Hong Kong at all but, rather, is transcribing rambling travellers' tales told to him by an old woman who has herself never been there. The last words of dying Lady Ava in the book's closing pages are a verdict on the world of the novel: 'Things are never set in order once and for all.'[8] *La Maison de rendez-vous* is perhaps the most extreme of French postmodern detective stories. Its contents are a collage of pulp-fiction stereotypes, taken from early twentieth-century orientalist crime thrillers like the Fu Manchu

---

stories. Robbe-Grillet's following novel, *Projet pour une révolution à New York* (*Project for a Revolution in New York*, 1970), would do much the same with the tropes of American *noir*. In the dreamlike chaos with which these contents are presented, the novel takes a despairing view of everything upon which the conventional genre relies– trustworthy perception, memory and reason, stable identity and accessible truth – while at the same time showing glimmers of sensual pleasure in the freedom afforded by the total breakdown of everything from the rules of morality to the rules of logic.

Robbe-Grillet's relationship to the traditional detective story is not an entirely destructive one, however. As with Butor, he takes inspiration from the genre's unique characteristics and, in particular, from the peculiar quality of its descriptive passages where everything we see may be a vital piece of the puzzle or a total irrelevancy. For Robbe-Grillet, this exempts crime fiction from the charge he lays at the door of traditional fiction of 'humanizing' the inanimate world by seeing it in terms of its role in a human drama. Thus, bars on a window traditionally stand for the impossibility of someone escaping; an empty chair means someone is absent or expected. In crime fiction, where we cannot be sure of what objects 'mean' for as long as the mystery persists, we come a step closer to seeing the true alienation of physical reality from human concerns.[9] The lesson Robbe-Grillet draws from crime fiction results in *chosisme,* his striking descriptive style which shows us ordinary objects in precise, sometimes geometric detail, but whose significance in the story remains obscure. The practice (which is, incidentally, echoed to some extent in Perec through his obsession with things too 'infra-ordinary' for us to notice) is to be found even in those of Robbe-Grillet's works which otherwise have little to do with crime fiction. It neatly demonstrates postmodern culture's openness to ideas from all spheres of artistic production, as well as the pervasive influence of crime fiction in even the most abstract questions of representation.

Recent postmodern crime fiction

Unlike the OuLiPo or New Novel detective stories, many contemporary examples of postmodern crime in French literature present little clear distinction between themselves and the 'straight' crime genre. Perec, Butor and company, for all their enthusiasm towards detective fiction, could never be mistaken for crime writers themselves, and anyone unfortunate enough to attempt a reading of their work on crime-fiction terms would end up frustrated and annoyed. However, in a list of producers of notable postmodern crime novels from the following generation, such as Sébastien Japrisot, Pascal Lainé, Daniel Pennac, Patrick Modiano, Julia Kristeva and Jean Echenoz, it proves impossible to draw a line dividing 'literary writers' from 'genre writers', something with which French publishing's strict classifications have had difficulty in dealing. Japrisot, for instance, began his career with a reasonably straightforward crime novel in *Compartiment Tueurs* (*The 10:30 from Marseille*, 1962), albeit one in which the culprit is the detective's sidekick. By *La Passion des femmes* (*Women in Evidence*, 1986), we have a final-chapter revelation that the hero's fatal wound is tomato juice, and that the entire contents of the novel have been a mixture of his vivid imagination and his memories of classic films, ending with his speculations as to his own possibly fictional status. Between these novels is an *oeuvre* in which the experimental techniques of the literary elite are brought into the service of traditional murder mysteries, with brilliant results. Japrisot's novels generally dispense with detectives and instead play with narrative perspective to create mysteries around the theme of identity. *L'Été meurtrier* (*One Deadly Summer*, 1977) divides its narrative between four narrators, showing us the protagonists by turns externally and from their own point of view as the reader gradually uncovers a tale of hidden motivations and deadly exploitation. *La Dame dans l'auto avec des lunettes et un fusil* (*The Lady in the Car with Glasses and a Gun*, 1966) takes us in and out of the subjective viewpoint of its heroine to tease us with the apparently impossible situation where, as she drives across France with a killer in pursuit and an unknown corpse in the boot of the car, everyone she meets claims to have met her before. Perhaps most interestingly of all, *Piège pour Cendrillon* (*Trap for Cinderella*, 1965) stays with the perspective of a single female narrator, the disfigured, amnesiac survivor of a fire which killed her stepsister, and builds the mystery out of the narrator's shifting suspicions over which of the two girls she might be, and whether she might be responsible for the other's death. The satisfying, if convoluted solutions offered at the denouement are sure to please traditionalist crime readers, while the perspectival play both harks back to the very earliest crime novels, such as Wilkie Collins's *The Woman in White* (1859) and *The Moonstone* (1868), and, in a typically postmodern move, puts the telling firmly at the forefront of the tale.

The two other writers on the list who can generally be relied upon to spin out and resolve a mystery in approved fashion are Pascal Lainé and Daniel Pennac. Lainé is the less interesting of the two, since he divides off his *comédies policières* – light-hearted Agatha Christie spoofs featuring the investigations of Miss Marple's nephew – from his 'serious' literary output like the prize-winning *La Dentellière* (1974). There is nevertheless some clever subversion of crime fiction convention to be had: for instance, in the first of the series, *Trois petits meurtres... et puis s'en va* (1985), the detective expounds the crime story and designates the culprit at the traditional reunion of suspects; in an epilogue, however, we discover that much of what he took to be the murderer's diabolical plan was in fact the actions of pure chance (as is also the case in Eco's *The Name of the Rose*), and that there may not have been a crime committed at all. Pennac's six Belleville novels, promoted mid-way through their run from Gallimard's Série Noire to its mainstream literary collection in recognition of their literary qualities, do have villains to be unmasked and truth and order to be restored at their denouements. They also, however, play around with crime formulas (the murder victims in one novel turn out to have committed suicide, for instance) and take place in such a surreal world that their implausibilities veer into parody. In one novel the heroine's aborted foetus is inserted into the uterus of another woman without her knowledge where it is brought to term. In another, the hero, Benjamin Malaussène, is harvested of his internal organs after having been shot through the brain and yet still manages to return unscathed for the happy ending and three further novels. Pennac's most postmodern characteristic, though, is that his detective stories are at least as much about stories as they are about detecting. Malaussène is above all else a storyteller; not only does he narrate each of the novels, he also attempts to get a (rather different) version of the first one published, allowing Pennac much scope for self-deprecating humour as his narrator's talents are comprehensively rubbished by the publisher: 'It's not what I'd call a book, it has no aesthetic plan, it heads off in all directions and goes nowhere. And you'll never manage anything better.'[10] Further self-reference comes when the novels start to retell their own stories within the world of the text. Mid-way through *Au bonheur des ogres* (*The Scapegoat*, 1985), a chapter opens with a police siege at the home of the prime suspect. But, as the episode develops, peculiar details accumulate. The police commissioner, who earlier in the story reminded Malaussène of Napoleon, now appears as a full-blown Bonaparte caricature, dressed in period costume, with hand in waistcoat and curl across forehead. When, a little later, cartoonish detectives Jib la Hyène and Pat les Pattes arrive, the game is up, and the episode is revealed as Malaussène's bedtime story to his younger siblings, offering them reassuring closure to the ongoing danger in their lives. As his listeners respond as junior literary critics, scouring the plot for logical flaws, Pennac is able to explore how mystery stories work within the bounds of his own mystery story, rather as Perec's or Butor's crime-fictions-within-fictions mirror our own reading process to us. Similar narrative games are played in *La Fée carabine* (*The Fairy Gunmother*, 1987), which loops around to enfold its own text as, in its final chapter, a character begins to re-narrate events using the novel's opening lines. And in *Monsieur Malaussène* (1995) we see Malaussène tried and condemned for twenty-one murders, before the episode is once again revealed to be doubly fictional, on this occasion, Malaussène's brother's 're-imagining' of his story. The eight 'fake' chapters which comprise this episode necessitate a long metafictional digression in their wake, as Malaussène sorts out true from false; engages in a discussion of the rights and duties of the narrator and accuses disgruntled readers of putting their desire for narrative coherence above their desire for justice. The Belleville novels' endless inventiveness and delight in the possibilities of storytelling have allowed Pennac to combine critical acclaim with immense popular success, perhaps also aided by his ability to maintain real emotional warmth amid all the postmodern cleverness.

The other three contemporary novelists mentioned earlier – Modiano, Kristeva and Echenoz – also offer us mysteries, but are less likely to satisfy readers who like their loose ends tied up neatly. Modiano and Kristeva stand a little apart from our other writers, in that their primary interest is neither in supplying the traditional pleasures of the well-made mystery nor in exploring the experimental possibilities to be found in subverting its formula. Rather, they are interested in questions of identity and human nature and find the detective-story form a useful medium through which to discuss them. Modiano's extensive *oeuvre* forms a pessimistic meditation on the fragility of the self, the inadequacy of memory and the irrecoverable nature of the past. Many of his novels make use of crime fiction for this. Two which engage particularly closely with the genre are *Quartier perdu* (*Trace of Malice*, 1984) and the prize-winning *Rue des boutiques obscures* (*Missing Person*, 1978). In each of these novels, the narrator, a crime writer in the former and a private detective in the latter, investigates into his own past, seeking out the people and places connected with a traumatic event in his youth. In *Rue des boutiques obscures*, as in *Piège pour Cendrillon*, the hero is an amnesiac; the past he uncovers is one in which, fleeing Nazi persecution, he was swindled and left for dead in the freezing Alps near the Swiss border. In *Quartier perdu*, the amnesia is voluntary, as the narrator has mentally blanked out his youth in Paris from where he fled after involvement in a shooting. His return to France twenty years later stirs memories and drives him to revisit the mysterious circumstances of the event. In both cases, the narrator's lack of a past leaves him with an incomplete identity and so he is not so much in search of facts about the past as in search of wholeness of the self. Both novels resolve their mystery to some extent at the denouement, while leaving some threads dangling. There is enough information to satisfy readerly curiosity, but not enough for the investigators to consider themselves successful. At the end of the novels, they remain fractured people and what they have learned from their detective work is not so much a sense of identity, but the futility of trying to recover one. And it is not only a futile pursuit, but also a harmful one. The narrator of *Rue des boutiques obscures* finds his way back to the site of his doomed escape into the mountains, but tells his taxi driver to turn back as they approach it. The final line of *Quartier perdu* has the narrator wishing he could forget everything. Instead of providing closure, their detective work has reawoken old pain and, as in *Les Gommes*, the quest for truth is depicted as having negative consequences.

We have the same renunciation and disillusion at the end of Kristeva's first detective novel, *Le Vieil homme et les loups* (*The Old Man and the Wolves*, 1991), since followed by two sequels. Kristeva, best known for her psychoanalysis-inspired post-structuralist theory, turns to the crime novel to dramatize some of her ideas on the darker side of human nature, as well as to find an oblique outlet for discussion of her own father's death, mirrored in the murder of the old man himself. The discourse of the novel slides from American *noir* to dreamlike surrealism, as the wolves of the title shift between metaphors for the characters' savagery and literal beasts roaming Santa Barbara in search of prey. As in many of the novels we have seen, an inconclusive plot structure reflects the pessimism of the novel's themes. At the end of the story, the narrator leaves Santa Barbara for Paris, with only vague suspicions to show for her investigations. What has ended her inquiries is the recognition, as with Modiano's narrators, that the task is beyond her; the truth too elusive to grasp and the wrongs too severe to be righted. But, in Kristeva's case, this renunciation also comes from a growing disgust with human nature. Having seen the violence and hatred beneath the surface of society, the narrator attempts to flee the entire sordid business, but is forced to acknowledge in the closing lines that the wolves are everywhere, even within herself.

The sixth and last of our contemporary writers, Jean Echenoz, is perhaps the most quintessentially postmodern of all. Certainly he is the one to whom the label has attached itself more indelibly than to any other writer mentioned here. He himself describes his early novels as homages to genre fiction – the *roman noir*, the spy novel, the adventure story, science fiction and disaster movies – and his more recent work, while no longer engaging so closely with popular culture, often retains some family resemblance to *noir* thrillers. Discussing his influences, he claims to owe almost everything to two writers, Raymond Queneau and Jean-Patrick Manchette, and his writing is indeed well characterized as a mixture of playful Oulipian inventiveness and the cool detachment of Manchette's violent crime novels.[11] Self-conscious allusions to crime fiction and its conventions abound in his work. *Le Méridien de Greenwich* (1979), for instance, lifts a character from the film version of Dashiell Hammett's classic *The Maltese Falcon*, insouciantly passing off as coincidence the identical name and appearance. *Cherokee* (1983), from which the extract below is taken, is a compendium of familiar *noir* tropes, brimming with femmes fatales, underworld crime bosses and mismatched police partner-ships, all set loose in a plot so filled with complexities and double bluffs that even the author admits to losing his way in it. The novel turns on the Ferro estate, an Alpine mansion forming part of an unclaimed inheritance, with treasure hidden in its grounds and a bizarre secret cult occupying the premises. Rival crooks plot to get their hands on the loot, while police and private detectives struggle to thwart them. As the large cast of characters play out their complex and violent intrigues, the reader can never be sure who is in league with whom or which apparently innocent events will turn out to be part of an elaborate set-up. The situation is exacerbated by an insouciantly deadpan narrator who thinks nothing of lingering over minor characters and irrelevant scenes while skipping over vital episodes, or neglecting the action to tell us about the music playing on the radio in the background, so erratic is his focus of attention. Even setting aside the manner of its telling, the tale itself is an eccentric one. Familiar *noir* devices are exaggerated into parody – as when the convergence of charac-ters at the Ferro mansion in the climax leads to no less than twelve dramatic entrances in the last forty pages – or ironically undercut, as when one character's long drive to make this dramatic entrance exhausts him so much that he sleeps through the final revelations and another misjudges his timing and bursts in to find everything is all over.

As in Perec and Robbe-Grillet, there is stylistic emphasis on the visual, drawing our attention to the ordinary. This often takes the form of striking visual metaphors – as we see in the extract with the unexpected appear-ance of a headless duck and a worm on speed to describe a road map in the wind – which resemble semi-parodic updatings of the colourful similes of Raymond Chandler's classic *noir*. Further evidence of the whimsical nature of Echenoz's narrative can be seen in the passage as he cheerfully highlights the pointlessness of the episode: there really was no good reason to attack the detectives and steal their car, which is, in any case, suffering from serious engine trouble and in no state to reach the Alps. In narrative terms, all the episode has achieved is to abort a potentially promising plotline, since all four characters must now return home and postpone the visit to the Ferro mansion until later in the novel. There is a gratuitousness to such plotting, but also a welcome element of the unexpected. Echenoz's disregard for the 'rules' of thriller development means that we can never feel confident about what will happen next. What is also arguably gratuitous is the violence in the extract, made all the more so by the jokey detachment with which the incident is recounted. Echenoz's work in general discourages the reader from identifying with or caring too much about the characters, a characteristic which lends weight to Fredric Jameson's views on the waning of emotional involvement in postmodern pastiche. Indeed, if Echenoz's homages engage the reader on an emotional level at all, it is in the communication of a certain melancholy at the superficiality and futility of the characters and their frenetic exertions. But these novels are not about feelings; they are irreverent play that gives us a fresh look at the crime fiction world and subverts the reader's expectations at every turn, even when we were not aware that we had expectations to subvert.

From Queneau to Echenoz, then, we have a half century of writers appropriating the themes, plots and characters of crime fiction to use or abuse them for their own purposes. Postmodern detectives in French culture are not limited to the novel, however. Postmodern crime stories of stage and screen include Eugène Ionesco's play *Tueur sans gages* (*A Gun for Free*, 1958), in which an insane, randomly striking serial killer becomes a metaphor for our mortality, New Wave films inspired by American B-movie thrillers, such as François Truffaut's *Tirez sur le pianiste* (1960) or Jean-Luc Godard's *A bout de souffle* (1960) or more recent films like François Ozon's twisty reflexive thriller, *Swimming Pool* (2003). Like the postmodern art of Warhol and Lichtenstein, the novels of Roubaud, Robbe-Grillet, Pennac and others present to us the familiar things of popular culture, but their grotesque exaggerations or unusual contexts throw new light on the material, making us look harder at what the conventional genre asks us to take for granted. Like postmodern architecture, postmodern crime fiction in its many guises plays with form and turns the detective story inside out, exposing the mechanics of its narrative to explore how literature functions. Like the novels and films of Fowles, Vonnegut, Lynch and Scott, postmodern crime fiction has elements of pastiche, imitating and transforming the genre without being reducible to the satirical aims of parody. Through these elements of pastiche, it is able to elaborate a metafictional commentary on its target and on the way we read it. And, echoing the ideas of postmodern thinkers, these authors flaunt the second-hand status of their 'simulacra' of crime fiction, deconstruct assumptions that the classic genre tends to conceal or turn a sceptical eye on truth and reason via their tales of failed investigations and insoluble crimes. For some people, like Jameson, these writers may have lost some vital humanity in their clever games and borrowed discourses. For others, they may display too much self-conscious intellectualism or too little respect for the traditions of the genre on which they are parasitic. But, for many people, postmodern detective stories offer intellectual pleasure, comic subversion and thought-provoking new perspectives. And if we are charitable enough to take this view, then we can find evidence in these works that crime fiction is a form robust and versatile enough to investigate the deepest aspects of human nature, to touch on abstract questions of the philosophy of knowledge and to inquire into the nature of fiction itself.

* * *

Extract from Jean Echenoz's *Cherokee*

Bock and Ripert, two detectives investigating the unclaimed fortune of the Ferro legacy, are at a service station en route for the Ferro mansion when Bock catches sight of George Chave, a former employee of the detective agency suspected of stealing the dossier on the Ferro case. George is also heading for the Ferro mansion, accompanied by the enigmatic British toothpaste millionaire, Ferguson Gibbs. George and Ferguson flee as Bock gives chase.

In their haste, George and Ferguson took the symmetrical escalator in the wrong direction, had to hurtle down the steps four times faster than they climbed. Bock absurdly tried to follow the same path, slipped on a step, caught himself on the rail, had to let himself be carried back up to the landing before rushing on to the stairs, lost time. He only emerged onto the parking lot in time to see, too far away, Chave and the redhead quickly open the doors to the Citroën, in which Ripert was until then peacefully smoking while consulting a road map unfolded on his knees. Bock saw George brutally yank Ripert from the car, saw Ripert fall with a short, frightened cry on the painted floor of the parking lot, his map unfurling over him, his neck sharply striking a cement abutment. Although Ripert had stopped moving, Bock saw the Englishman run around the car to administer two or three furtive kicks. Then the road map gained a sort of momentum under the feeble wind, crawling on its belly in spasmodic creasings like a giant earthworm on Benzedrine, with a mechanical, frozen rhythm suggesting the posthumous sprint of a decapitated duck. George dove behind the steering wheel, followed by the redhead, who jumped into the back seat of the yellow car.

Jean Echenoz, *Cherokee* (1983), trans. Mark Polizzotti (London: Faber and Faber, 1991), pp. 110–11.

Notes

1. For accessible English-language introductions to each of these thinkers, see Simon Malpas, *Jean-François Lyotard* (London: Routledge, 2003); Richard J. Lane, *Jean Baudrillard* (London: Routledge, 2000); and Nicholas Royle, *Jacques Derrida* (London: Routledge, 2003).

2. Umberto Eco, *Reflections on the Name of the Rose*, trans. William Weaver (London: Secker and Warburg, 1985), p. 67.

3. Fredric Jameson, *Postmodernism, or, the Cultural Logic of Late Capitalism* (London: Verso, 1991), pp. 1–54.

4. 'Il voyait le roman que cela aurait pu faire, un roman policier avec un crime, un coupable et un détective, et … il voyait le roman que cela avait fait, un roman si dépouillé d'artifice qu'il n'était point possible de savoir s'il y avait une énigme à résoudre ou s'il n'y en avait pas, un roman où tout aurait pu s'enchaîner suivant des plans de police, et, en fait, parfaitement dégarni de tous les plaisirs que provoque le spectacle, une activité de cet ordre', pp. 210–11.

5. See the 'histoire du diplomate suédois' ('the story of the Swedish diplomat') in chapter 31, the 'histoire de l'acteur qui simula sa mort' ('the story of the actor who faked his own death') in chapter 34, and the 'histoire du bijoutier qui fut assassiné trois fois' ('the story of the jeweller who was murdered three times') in chapter 50.

6. See Tzvetan Todorov, *The Poetics of Prose*, trans. Richard Howard (Oxford: Blackwell, 1977), pp. 42–52.

7. 'Je vais donc essayer maintenant de raconter cette soirée chez Lady Ava, de préciser en tout cas quels furent, à ma connaissance, les principaux événements qui l'ont marquée. Je suis arrivé à la Villa Bleue vers neuf heures dix, en taxi', pp. 23–4.

8. 'Les choses ne sont jamais définitivement en ordre', p. 209.

9. See Robbe-Grillet's essay, 'Une voie pour le roman futur' (1956), in *Pour un nouveau roman* (Paris: Minuit, 1961).

10. 'Ce n'est pas un livre, ça, il n'y a aucun projet esthétique, là-dedans, ça part dans tous les sens et ça ne mène nulle part. Et vous ne ferez jamais mieux', *Au bonheur des ogres* , pp. 266–7.

¹¹ Jean Echenoz, 'Neuf notes sur *Fatale*', postface to Jean-Patrick Manchette, *Fatale* (Paris: Gallimard, 1996), pp. 147–54.

Select bibliography

Butor, Michel, *L'Emploi du temps* (Paris: Minuit, 1956). *Passing Time*, trans. Jean Stewart (London: Calder, 1961).

Desnos, Robert, 'La Complainte de Fantômas' (1933), in *Œuvres*, ed. Marie-Claire Dumas (Paris: Gallimard, 1999), pp. 944–49.

Echenoz, Jean, *Le Méridien de Greenwich* (Paris: Minuit, 1979).

—— *Cherokee* (Paris: Minuit, 1983). *Cherokee*, trans. Mark Polizzotti (London: Faber and Faber, 1991).

Japrisot, Sébastien, *Compartiment Tueurs* (Paris: Denoël, 1962). *The 10:30 from Marseille*, trans. Francis Price (London: Souvenir Press, 1964).

—— *Piège pour Cendrillon* (Paris: Denoël, 1965). *Trap for Cinderella*, trans. Helen Weaver (London: Souvenir Press, 1965).

—— *La Dame dans l'auto avec des lunettes et un fusil* (Paris: Denoël, 1966). *The Lady in the Car with Glasses and a Gun*, trans. Helen Weaver (Harpenden: No Exit, 1989).

—— *L'Été meurtrier* (Paris: Denoël, 1977). *One Deadly Summer*, trans. Alan Sheridan (London: Secker and Warburg, 1980).

—— *La Passion des femmes* (Paris: Denoël, 1986). *Women in Evidence*, trans. Ros Schwartz (London: Secker and Warburg, 1990).

Kristeva, Julia, *Le Vieil homme et les loups* (Paris: Fayard, 1991). *The Old Man and the Wolves*, trans. Barbara Bray (New York: Columbia University Press, 1994).

Lainé, Pascal, *Trois petits meurtres... et puis s'en va* (Paris: Ramsay, 1985).

Modiano, Patrick, *Rue des boutiques obscures* (Paris: Gallimard, 1978). *Missing Person*, trans. Daniel Weissbort (London: Cape, 1980).

—— *Quartier perdu* (Paris: Gallimard, 1984). *A Trace of Malice*, trans. Anthea Bell (Nuffield: Aidan Ellis, 1988).

Pennac, Daniel, *Au bonheur des ogres* (Paris: Gallimard, 1985). *The Scapegoat*, trans. Ian Monk (London: Harvill, 1999).

—— *La Fée carabine* (Paris: Gallimard, 1987). *The Fairy Gunmother*, trans. Ian Monk (London: Harvill, 1997).

—— *Monsieur Malaussène* (Paris: Gallimard, 1995). *Monsieur Malaussène*, trans. Ian Monk (London: Harvill, 2003).

Perec, Georges, *La Disparition* (Paris: Denoël, 1969). *A Void*, trans. Gilbert Adair (London: Harvill, 1994).

—— *Les Revenentes* (Paris: Julliard, 1972). 'The Exeter Text: Jewels, Secrets, Sex', trans. Ian Monk, in *Three by Perec* (London: Harvill, 1996).

—— *La Vie mode d'emploi* (Paris: Hachette, 1978). *Life, a User's Manual*, trans. David Bellos (London: Harvill, 1988).

—— *'53 jours'* (Paris: Gallimard, 1989). *'53 Days'*, trans. David Bellos (London: Harvill, 1992).

Queneau, Raymond, *Pierrot mon ami* (Paris: Gallimard, 1942). *Pierrot mon ami*, trans. Barbara Wright (London: Atlas, 1988).

Robbe-Grillet, Alain, *Les Gommes* (Paris: Minuit, 1953). *The Erasers*, trans. Richard Howard (London: Calder, 1966).

—— *La Maison de rendez-vous* (Paris: Minuit, 1965). *The House of Assignation*, trans. A. M. Sheridan Smith (London: Calder, 1970).

—— *Projet pour une révolution à New York* (Paris: Minuit, 1970). *Project for a Revolution in New York*, trans. Richard Howard (London: Calder, 1973).

Roubaud, Jacques, *La Belle Hortense* (Paris: Ramsay, 1985).

Further secondary reading

Bellos, David, *Georges Perec: A Life in Words* (London: Harvill, 1993).

Best, Victoria, 'Life beyond death: reading for the demonic in the texts of Modiano and Japrisot', *French Studies*, 60 (2006), 218–31.

Davis, Colin, and Elizabeth Fallaize, *French Fiction in the Mitterrand Years: Memory, Narrative, Desire* (Oxford: Oxford University Press, 2000).

Fletcher, John, *Alain Robbe-Grillet* (London: Methuen, 1983).

Jameson, Fredric, *Postmodernism, or, the Cultural Logic of Late Capitalism* (London: Verso, 1991).

Jefferson, Ann, *The Nouveau Roman and the Poetics of Fiction* (Cambridge: Cambridge University Press, 1980).

Kemp, Simon, *Defective Inspectors: Crime Fiction Pastiche in Late-Twentieth-Century French Literature* (Oxford: Legenda, 2006).

Nettelbeck, Colin W., 'The "post-literary" novel: Echenoz, Pennac and company', *French Cultural Studies*, 5/2 (1994), 113–38.

Thompson, William (ed.), *The Contemporary Novel in France* (Gainsville, FL: University Press of Florida, 1995).

Waugh, Patricia, *Metafiction: The Theory and Practice of Self-Conscious Fiction* (London: Methuen, 1984).

Conclusion

CLAIRE GORRARA

This volume has demonstrated the rich and multifaceted nature of French crime fiction as a literary form. As popular culture, French crime fiction infiltrates and traverses many arenas of cultural activity, reaching a diverse readership attracted to its thematic preoccupations with crime, transgression and human fallibility and the formal set of conventions and structures within which these are explored. Whether cast as the murder-mystery, the *roman noir*, the thriller or suspense novel, French and francophone crime fiction has exhibited a capacity to change and respond to new demands and expectations, both producing pioneering authors and creations and engaging in productive dialogues with other forms and media of popular culture. Yet, as this volume attests, a number of French authors have also challenged ingrained and highly polarized high/low cultural divides which present such popular genres as purely formulaic, repetitive and lacking in literary merit. From its oblique affiliations with surrealism to contemporary postmoderism, crime fiction has offered selected French writers the generic frames within which to further the quest for literary experimentation and innovation.

If the varied sub-genres of French crime fiction have provided a rich terrain for stylistic play and reformulation, they have equally generated narratives of social engagement and critique, with crime as a privileged optic on contemporary French realities. This is evident in a number of essays in this collection and examined in a range of forms and contexts, such as the earliest French crime narratives and their questioning of scientific rationalism, the political charge of the *néo-polar* and its explosive denunciations of late twentieth-century capitalism and the contribution of women crime writers and their dismantling of the sexist assumptions upon which much crime fiction and its criticism resides. In its myriad manifestations, some of the best French crime writing has consistently drawn upon 'topical' issues of the day and provided an often incisive analysis of the ills of the nation, diagnosing the rotten state of affairs within French society, its institutions and the state.

This national specificity should not detract, however, from the ways in which French crime fiction has been influenced by transnational exchanges and debates, above all a transatlantic circuit shaped by relations with America and Britain. Such a circuit is central to a number of chapters in this volume. Founded at the intersection of three cultures in the mid-nineteenth century and open to cross-cultural traffic both within and beyond the francophone world, forms of French crime fiction have been, and remain, attentive to the shifts and transformation of crime fiction as a global phenomenon. Impelled by the growth of the mass media, French crime fiction has proved itself ever adaptable to changing contexts, both appropriating 'foreign' models, such as hard-boiled crime fiction, for French readers and acting itself as a cultural mediator for such forms to take root in wider European culture.

Into the twenty-first century, which new directions and trends may be charted for such a protean and responsive form of literary fiction? First, it is clear that crime fiction is fast securing a place for itself as a valued part of France's cultural heritage. As Annie Collovald and Erik Neveu have claimed recently, crime fiction in France can now aspire to the critical recognition and cultural cachet that has been long denied it.[1] In France, as elsewhere, the boundaries demarcating popular and so-called literary fiction are far less distinct than in the past and this cultural reordering is nowhere more evident than in the changing reception of crime fiction. A number of highly regarded French writers who began their careers as crime writers have, in later years, achieved literary fame and success as critically acclaimed mainstream authors. Sébastien Japrisot, Daniel Pennac and Jean Vautrin have all received literary plaudits for their fiction, published and marketed outside popular crime fiction collections.[2] The phenomenon of what we might call the 'cross-over' crime writer is not unique to France and has been discussed by British crime critics, such as Mark Lawson. Lawson, in common with other exasperated reviewers of crime fiction in the mainstream British press, berates a tendency to categorize crime writing as somehow inferior writing practice. He cites the example of Man Booker prizewinner John Banville who has gone on to write two detective novels under the name of Benjamin Black, following his critical success with *The Sea* in 2005. Lawson notes the productive coexistence of Banville's different writing personae and styles and makes a strong case for the intertwining of the 'literary' and the 'populist' in his work and the persistence of features common to both in terms of plot and characterization.[3] Indeed, as best-seller French crime writer Fred Vargas has argued, contemporary crime fiction has offered a haven for storytellers, those 'refugees' from structuralist assaults on the realist novel in the 1960s and 1970s. Far from operating as a lesser form of literary activity, it is crime fiction that has come to the rescue of French literary traditions at times of crisis, nurturing the art of storytelling and reinvigorating the cultural sphere.[4]

Secondly, the production and dissemination of French crime fiction is increasing at an accelerated rate, allowing a new generation of French novelists to reach a wide readership. Since the early 1990s, a number of specialist publishing houses and new crime fiction collections have sprouted up in France. Publishing ventures, such as L'Écailler du sud, Éditions Jigal and Éditions Baleine (the latter having undergone a number of editorial transformations), cater specifically for the demands of a voracious crime fiction readership, whilst collections such as Éditions Viviane Hamy's Chemins Nocturnes or Éditions Métailié's Suites Noir and Romans Noirs have launched the careers of major French talents and acted as the powerhouses for the promotion of contemporary French crime fiction. Important features of such a reconfigured publishing landscape are the focus on 'regional' French crime fiction, above all from the south of France and the city of Marseille, and a preoccupation with crime fiction's relationship to narratives of city space, place and identity. The latter is perhaps best exemplified by Éditions Autrement's collection Noir Urbain in which a phototextual narrative is created by the intersections of text and photograph as a crime story unfolds in a precise urban location – city, district, even street.[5] In addition, the Internet has been a highly significant forum for the promotion of new French crime fiction, with specialist websites and blogs offering 'word of mouth' updates on authors, their works and forthcoming film adaptations and translations.[6]

Thirdly, recent years have witnessed a significant upturn in the cultural flow of crime fiction from the francophone world to the anglophone world, counterbalancing, to some small degree, the enormous disparities of much of the past century. Interest in translations of French and francophone crime novels into English has been revitalized by the phenomenal success of Fred Vargas, in terms of both sales figures and critical acclaim. Vargas has twice been awarded the coveted Duncan Lawrie International Dagger for the best crime novel translated into English from another language, an unprecedented feat.[7] Her exposure to anglophone readers can be attributed in part to the support of pioneering editors, such as Christopher MacLehose, formerly editor of Harvill Press and now with Quercus as editor of the MacLehose Press imprint. MacLehose has been instrumental in the translation and marketing of a range of European crime writers to British and American readers, including Henning Mankell, Daniel Pennac and Massimo Carlotti. Whilst it is difficult to determine the model of French crime fiction that has attracted anglophone translators and editors in recent years, it would appear that there is a marked preference for historical crime fiction, set in culturally resonant contexts, which showcase the specialist knowledge of the authors themselves.[8] Contemporary French *noir* has a place in such cultural transfers, particularly the work of Dominique Manotti, but to a far lesser degree, indicating the prevalent cultural imaginings of the French 'Other' for British and American crime fiction readers: cultivated, erudite and a champion of Enlightenment values.

In conclusion, this dialogue between anglophone and francophone crime cultures looks set to continue apace. Cross-cultural publications, such as the recent short story collection *Paris Noir: Capital Crime Fiction* presenting French, British and American-authored crime fiction set in Paris, demonstrate the ongoing fascination with Paris, and France more generally, as the locus of criminality and transgression.[9] Such texts gesture at the persistent, if sometimes unacknowledged, influence of French crime writing traditions on anglophone authors, even if the current flow of traffic is not set to be reversed any time soon. Within French and francophone cultures more widely, however, signs are propitious that crime fiction is entering a period of growth as key proponents and practitioners seize the initiative to promote the value and appeal of popular forms of fiction at a vital juncture in French cultural history. The time may well be ripe to 'break down the wall of condescension which separates the kind of fiction that is set for exams and given prizes from the kind that sells in supermarkets and has clues and a solution'.[10] This publication stands as testament to such an aspiration.

Notes

[1] Annie Collovald and Erik Neveu, *Lire le noir: enquête sur les lecteurs de récits policiers* (Paris: Bibliothèque publique d'information/Centre Pompidou. 2004) describe this phenomenon as crime fiction taking 'l'ascenseur vers la légitimité culturelle' (the lift upwards towards cultural legitimacy), p. 16.

[2] See, most recently, Daniel Pennac's attribution of the Prix Renaudot 2007 for *Chagrins d'école*.

[3] Mark Lawson, 'Populist prejudice', *Guardian*, 25 January 2008.

[4] Nicholas Wroe, 'Grave concerns – interview with Fred Vargas', *Guardian*, 16 February 2008.

[5] In the catalogue of Éditions Autrement, the collection Noir Urbain is defined as presenting 'un lieu précis, un auteur, un photographe: petits romans noirs de

quartiers d'aujourd'hui' (a precise location, an author, a photographer: short *romans noirs* from today's cities).

[6] Of the various sites available, one of the most useful for those interested in European crime fictions is *http://internationalnoir.blogspot.com.*

[7] The two novels awarded the International Dagger were (in translation): (2006) *The Three Evangelists* (Harvill Press) and (2007*) Wash This Blood Clean From My Hand* (Harvill/Secker).

[8] Most prominent of these French authors translated into English are Fred Vargas, a widely published historian and archaeologist who has written on medieval social structures and the epidemiology of the plague, and Jean-François Parot, currently French Ambassador to Guinea-Bissau and a specialist of eighteenth-century Paris.

[9] M. Jakubowski (ed.), *Paris Noir: Capital Crime Fiction* (London: Serpent's Tail, 2007). The cultural dominance of Anglo-American crime fiction is signalled by the fact that, of the eighteen stories, only five are by French authors.

[10] Lawson, 'Populist prejudice'.

Annotated Bibliography of Criticism on French Crime Fiction

CLAIRE GORRARA

This bibliography provides an overview of secondary sources devoted to the study of French crime fiction. It is intended as a starting point for research and focuses on full-length studies, specialist journals and special issues and useful French-language websites. The aim is to introduce readers to established studies and general overviews, in both French and English, which devote substantial chapters to French authors, novels, characters and writing contexts. In addition, an indispensable resource for researchers of French crime fiction is the Bibliothèque des littératures policières (Bilipo), located at 48–50, rue du Cardinal Lemoine, 75005 Paris. This is a specialist library devoted to detective and crime fiction and film, criminology and crime reporting. It is the copyright depository for all such published material in France and is active in supporting both pedagogical and more research-orientated ventures relating to crime narratives in a French context.

Full-length studies

Amey, Claude, *Jurifiction: roman policier et rapport juridique* (Paris: L'Harmattan, 1994): A well-argued narratological examination of detective and crime fiction.

Aziza, Claude, and Anne Rey, *La Littérature policière* (Paris: Les Guides Pocket Classiques, 2003): A well-focused chronological overview of crime fiction aimed at student and undergraduate audiences who may have had limited exposure to criticism on crime fiction. It uses well-chosen extracts to encourage the reader to explore further. The chapter on 'l'exception française' is particularly recommended.

Baudou, Jacques and Jean-Jacques Scheleret, *Le Polar* (Paris: Larousse, 2001): A rich compendium of crime fiction, film, *bande dessinée*, radio and television across francophone, European and anglophone cultures.

Bevenuti, Stefano, Gianni Rizzoni and Michel Lebrun, *Le Roman criminel: histoire, auteurs, personnages* (Nantes: L'Atalante, 1982): A well-conceived illustrated survey of crime fiction with a preface by Jean-Patrick Manchette. It inserts French traditions into wider frames with chapters entitled 'De Simenon à San Antonio' and 'La Nouvelle Génération en France', the latter focusing on the *néo-polar* school of writing.

Bilipo, *Les Crimes de l'année* (Paris: Bibliothèque des littératures policières): In existence since 1985, this annual survey of crime fiction published in French is an exceptionally good resource for those who wish either to research particular themes and debates and/or also identify the early critical reception of crime fiction published in France over the last twenty years.

Blanc, Jean-Noël, *Polarville: images de la ville dans le roman policier* (Lyon: Presses Universitaires de Lyon, 1991): An original examination of the representation of city space in crime fiction with considerable attention given to French authors.

Boileau-Narcejac, *Le Roman policier* (Paris: Quadrige/Presses Universitaires de France, 1975): A polemical survey of crime fiction from the detective-fiction duo Boileau-Narcejac. It makes a strong case for the intellectual primacy of classic detective fiction.

Bourdieu, Jean, *Histoire du roman policier* (Paris: Éditions de Fallois, 1996): A chronological survey of developments in crime fiction with a strong emphasis on shifts in form and theme.

Colin, Jean-Paul, *Le Roman policier archaïque: un essai de lecture groupée* (Berne: Peter Lang, 1984): Narratological analysis of early French crime fiction.

Colin, Jean-Paul, *Crimologies* (Saint Imier: Canevas Éditeur, 1995): A stimulating narratological exploration of structures and forms, focusing almost exclusively on French crime fictions.

Collovald, Annie, and Erik Neveu, *Lire le noir: enquête sur les lecteurs de récits policiers* (Bibliothèque publique d'information/Centre Pompidou, 2004): This sociologically inspired study provides a rich overview of the production, transmission and reception of *noir* crime fiction in France, using reader surveys and interviews to good effect.

Deleuse, Robert, *Les Maîtres du roman policier* (Paris: Bordas, 1991): An encyclopaedic survey of key crime fiction authors, including a high proportion of French figures.

Dubois, Jacques, *Le Roman policier ou la modernité* (Paris: Éditions Nathan, 1992): Excellent study of forms, structures and history of francophone traditions of detective and crime fiction with a close reading of three authors and their creations: Gaston Leroux, Georges Simenon and Sébastien Japrisot.

Dulout, Stéphanie, *Le Roman policier* (Toulouse: Les Essentiels Milan, 1995): A short chronological and thematic overview of crime fiction with French authors well represented.

Eisenzweig, Uri, *Le Récit impossible: sens et forme du roman policier* (Paris: Christian Bourgeois Éditeur, 1986): One of the most innovative analyses of early French detective fiction and its interpretative possibilities.

Evrard, Franck, *Lire le roman policier* (Paris: Dunod, 1996): An introductory survey of crime fiction aimed at an undergraduate audience with highlights including a useful appendix on key authors and terms.

Fernandez Recatela, Denis, *Le Polar* (Paris: MA Éditions, 1986): A bio-bibliography of key crime fiction authors, texts and characters.

Fondanèche, Daniel, *Le Roman policier* (Paris: Ellipses Éditions, 2000): This synthetic overview of the development of crime fiction from Poe to postmodernism includes chapters on 'le monde francophone de l'âge d'or', 'le temps du néo-polar' and 'l'école française'.

Fosca, François, *Histoire et technique du roman policier* (Éditions de la Nouvelle Revue Critique, 1937): An early study of detective and crime fiction, this text is richly discursive and persuasive in its analysis of representative authors, themes and figures.

Fosca, François, *Raisons d'aimer: les romans policiers* (Paris: Wesnael-Charlier, 1964): A personal appreciation of detective and crime fiction from one of the earliest francophone critics.

Gorrara, Claire, *The Roman Noir in Post-War French Culture: Dark Fictions* (Oxford: Oxford University Press, 2003): A study of the post-war French *roman noir* from its origins during the Second World War to the present day. Selected texts are read alongside specific historical contexts.

Hoveyda, Fereydoun, *Petite Histoire du roman policier* (Éditions du Pavillon, 1956): An early scholarly study of different models of detective fiction, including a preface by Jean Cocteau.

Lacassin, Francis, *Mythologie du roman policier* (Paris: Union Générale d'Éditions, 1974): A classic two-volume study of the mythic origins of detective and crime fiction that remains a major reference work in the field.

Lebrun, Michel and Jean-Paul Schweighaeuser, *Le Guide du polar: histoire du roman policier français* (Paris: Syros, 1987): A valuable survey of French and francophone traditions published at a time when criticism on French crime fiction was beginning to develop an academic profile.

Lits, Marc, *Le Roman policier: introduction à la théorie et à l'histoire d'un genre littéraire* (Liège: Éditions du Céfal, 1999): A comprehensive introduction to the structures, forms and history of francophone detective and crime fiction.

Mesplède, Claude (ed.), *Dictionnaire des littératures policières*, vols 1 and 2 (Nantes: Joseph K., 2007): An indispensable reference work comprising essential information on crime fiction writers, characters, themes, magazines and collections with a major focus on francophone writers and contexts.

Müller, Elfriede, and Alexander Ruoff, *Le Polar français: crime et histoire* (Paris: La Fabrique Éditions, 2002): A rich study of the relationship between post-war French crime fiction and recent history.

Narcejac, Thomas, *Esthétique du roman policier* (Paris: Le Portulan, 1947): An early analysis of the structures and forms of classic detective fiction.

Narcejac, Thomas, *Une machine à lire: le roman policier* (Paris: Denoël/Gonthier, 1975): A well-known defence of the *roman-problème* or classic detective fiction by one of French crime fiction's most accomplished post-war critics and writers.

Périsset, Maurice, *Panorama des maîtres du polar français contemporain* (Paris: L'Instant, 1986): A useful bio-bibliographical survey of French crime writers active in the 1980s.

Reuter, Yves, *Le Roman policier* (Paris: Nathan, 1997): A well-conceived introduction to the study of detective and crime fiction aimed at undergraduate students.

Schweighaeuser, Jean-Paul, *Le Roman noir français* (Paris: Presses Universitaires de France, 1984), collection Que sais-je?: A wide-ranging and informative analysis of French and francophone traditions of the *roman noir.*

Tourteau, Jean-Jacques, *D'Arsène Lupin à San Antonio: le roman policier français de 1900 à 1970* (Paris: Mame, 1970): A chronological overview of French crime fiction with a focus on key authors and their creations, ending with a series of extracts.

Tulard, Jean, *Dictionnaire du roman policier, 1841–2005* (Paris: Fayard, 2005): This bio-bibliographical survey sets out a selection of authors, collections and individual novels.

Vanoncini, André, *Le Roman policier* (Paris: Presses Universitaires de France, 1993), collection Que sais-je?: A well-received university treatment of crime fiction that gives admirable attention to European writers, including extensive reference to French authors.

Verdaguer, Pierre, *La Séduction policière: signes de croissance d'un genre réputé mineur* (Birmingham, Alabama: Summa Publications Inc., 1999): An examination of French crime fiction since the 1970s, addressing issues such as the portrayal of society, the contribution of women writers and the representation of history.

Selected specialist journals and special issues

French Cultural Studies, 12/3 (October 2001) 'Crime and punishment: narratives of order and disorder': A rich special issue devoted to discourses of crime and punishment with several contributions examining French crime fictions.

Les Temps modernes, 595 (August–October 1997), 'Pas d'orchidées pour les T.M.': A special issue of this prestigious intellectual review devoted to the *roman noir* with authoritative articles, interviews and short fiction.

Littérature, 49 (February 1983): An excellent series of academic essays on crime and detective fiction, notable too for a short interview with Jean-Patrick Manchette entitled 'Réponses'.

Magazine Littéraire has devoted a number of special issues to crime fiction, the most notable are: June 1986 (344) 'Le Planète polar' (section on France); August 1968 (20) with a 'petit dictionnaire des auteurs' with a strong French component; April 1983 (194) including Jean-Pierre Deloux's excellent analysis of the *néo-polar* phenomenon.

Mouvements, 15–16 (May–August 2001), 'Le Polar: entre critique sociale et désenchantement': A special issue devoted to crime fiction and social history with thought-provoking contributions, particularly on the *néo-polar* school of writing.

Polar (Paris: Rivages): Published from 1990 to 2001, this was one of the premier journals devoted to French and world crime fiction with invaluable specialist dossiers.

Temps noir: revue des littératures policières (Nantes: Éditions Joseph K.): Founded in 1998, this specialist review of crime fiction has an international focus with a good proportion of articles devoted to French and francophone novelists.

Yale French Studies, 108 (2005), 'Crime fictions': A wide-ranging special issue with articles devoted to French crime fictions from the nineteenth century to the contemporary period.

813: les amis de la littérature policière: Launched in 1980 together with an association of the same name, this crime magazine/fanzine is named after one of the adventures of Maurice Leblanc's turn-of-the-century gentleman-thief, Arsène Lupin. The magazine contains both generalist surveys and interviews and also devotes special issues to key figures and themes in world and French and francophone crime fiction.

Websites

There is a wealth of websites that include critical material on French detective and crime fiction. However, these can have a rather ephemeral existence. Noted below is a representative selection of those French-language sites active in 2007:

Europolar: *http://perso.orange.fr/arts.sombres/polar/edito_angl.htm*: A European venture devoted above all to *noir* crime fiction, this site is translated into five languages and includes scholarly articles as well as more generic book reviews and discussions.

A l'ombre du polar: *www.polars.org*: A French website devoted to crime fiction with features such as historical overviews, special dossiers, books reviews and mini-biographies.

Le Récit policier d'expression française: *http://membres.lycos.fr/bernadac/*: A well-informed website with in-depth authorial profiles and significant articles on key features and features of francophone detective and crime fiction.

Cercle noir: *www.cerclenoir.com*: A good source of information for current events, festivals and other information relating to French crime fiction.

Le Rayon du polar: *www.rayonnoir.com*: Primarily useful for information and reviews of newly published books, graphic novels and films in French relating to crime fiction.

L'Ours polar: *http://www.ours-polar.com/*: Primarily an association for the promotion of *noir* crime fiction, *ours polar* ventures also include a specialist journal, published biannually, workshops, literary salons and school activities, all designed to bring *noir* writing to greater public attention.

Index